"I'M GLAD YOU DON'T THINK I'M A WITCH, AS DID THAT MISGUIDED ZEALOT."

Cimarron smiled down at Lucinda as she put her arm through his. "Witches are said to be old and ugly; you're young and pretty."

Lucinda pouted. "I can be evil, though."

"Witch-evil?" asked a surprised Cimarron, as he ran a hand over her luscious arm. "You mean cast spells on people? Make them do bad things?"

Lucinda stopped walking and turned to face him. "I have been seriously considering putting a spell on you, Cimarron." She deliberately unbuttoned the top buttons of his shirt.

Cimarron laughed and finished what she started. "I don't need no witchy-woman to cast a spell on me to make me do *those* kinds of bad things. . . ."

CIMARRON AND THE HIGH RIDER

SIGNET Westerns You'll Enjoy

CIMARRON
AND THE HIGH RIDER

BY

LEO P. KELLEY

A SIGNET BOOK

NEW AMERICAN LIBRARY

PUBLISHER'S NOTE

This novel is a work of fiction. Names, characters, places, and incidents either are the product of the author's imagination or are used fictitiously, and any resemblance to actual persons, living or dead, or events is entirely coincidental.

NAL BOOKS ARE AVAILABLE AT QUANTITY DISCOUNTS WHEN USED TO PROMOTE PRODUCTS OR SERVICES. FOR INFORMATION PLEASE WRITE TO PREMIUM MARKETING DIVISION, THE NEW AMERICAN LIBRARY, INC., 1633 BROADWAY, NEW YORK, NEW YORK 10019.

The first chapter of this book appeared in *Cimarron and the Bounty Hunters*, the sixth volume in this series.

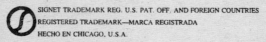

SIGNET TRADEMARK REG. U.S. PAT. OFF. AND FOREIGN COUNTRIES
REGISTERED TRADEMARK—MARCA REGISTRADA
HECHO EN CHICAGO, U.S.A.

SIGNET, SIGNET CLASSIC, MENTOR, PLUME, MERIDIAN and NAL BOOKS are published by The New American Library, Inc., 1633 Broadway, New York, New York 10019

First Printing, January, 1984

1 2 3 4 5 6 7 8 9

PRINTED IN THE UNITED STATES OF AMERICA

CIMARRON . . .

. . . he was a man with a past he wanted to forget and a future uncertain at best and dangerous at worst. Men feared and secretly admired him. Women desired him. He roamed the Indian Territory with a Winchester '73 in his saddle scabbard, an Army Colt in his hip holster, and a bronc he had broken beneath him. He packed his guns loose, rode his horse hard, and no one dared throw gravel in his boots. Once he had an ordinary name like other men. But a tragic killing forced him to abandon it and he became known only as Cimarron. *Cimarron*, in Spanish, meant wild and unruly. It suited him. *Cimarron*.

As he rode along the northern bank of the winding Arkansas
River, Cimarron took off his flat-topped black stetson
and wiped his forehead with the back of his hand. It came
away sweaty.

He clapped his hat back on his head and used the blue
bandanna that was tied around his neck to wipe the sweat
from the rest of his face.

His cotton shirt clung to him, its blueness turned black
because of the sweat that was oozing from his chest, back,
and arms.

In the sky above him, the early-morning August sun blazed,
unchallenged by a single cloud. Beneath his horse's hooves the
buffalo grass grew lushly as a result of its partnership with
the hot sun and the fertile earth, which had been soaked by a
heavy rain the night before.

As he rode into the small settlement of Parson's Point, his
eyes roved to the small house that was set far back from the
narrow dirt street. He found himself wondering if she were
home, and as if in answer to his speculation, Jenny Marlow's
head and shoulders appeared in a ground-floor window.

When she saw him, she waved wildly.

Cimarron returned her wave and then rode out of Parson's
Point toward the Cookson Hills, thinking of Jenny and all that
they had done together during their ardent meetings in the
too-distant past and of how she had done it all as wildly as

she had just waved at him. He smiled—and almost turned the black beneath him.

But visiting Jenny was one thing. Courting her, if that was the name for what he did when they were together, was always a rewarding experience. Cimarron's smile broadened. But courting a run-in with her father and her three burly brothers . . . His smile died.

The last time he had been in Parson's Point the four Marlow males had almost caught him with Jenny as they dallied in the thick clover growing in a secluded spot near the river. That had been a close one, he recalled. A whole lot too close for comfort. He was sure he could take on two of the Marlows at a time if that ever became necessary, but he was just as sure that he couldn't take on more than two at a time. Every one of them—the old man, Case Marlow, and the three brothers, Bart, the eldest, Jamie, the middle one, and Sooner, the youngest—was built as broad as a four-seated outhouse.

Cimarron rode on, reminiscing about Jenny, letting the black set its own slow pace since he was in no particular hurry to get back to Fort Smith, where Marshal Upham would, no doubt about it, have some new assignment to hand him.

But would he? Cimarron suddenly wondered. Maybe Upham wouldn't want him working as a deputy marshal because of the way he had set out to collect the bounty Harriet Becker had offered him without so much as a by-your-leave. Marshal Upham, he knew, could be testy. At times temperamental.

Cimarron absently patted the pocket of his jeans, which held the thousand dollars in bounty money he had collected. He nodded thoughtfully, thinking that the money would help him hold out for a time if Upham asked him to turn in his badge.

The money was a consolation, no doubt about that. But Cimarron was aware that his thoughts had made him uncomfortable. Why? The answer was obvious to him. Because he liked being a lawman—an officer of the District Court for the Western District of Arkansas. Being a lawman made him feel——how? Like I've got me a place in the world, he decided finally. Like I'm not just some fiddle-footed drifter dreaming dreams that probably won't ever come true while wandering all over creation looking for the pot of gold that's supposed to be sitting at the end of a rainbow somewhere.

He rode on, decidedly uneasy now and on the verge of regretting his earlier hasty departure from Fort Smith to set out after what had been, he now clearly realized, his own particular version of the pot of gold at the end of the rainbow.

By midafternoon he was in sight of Fort Smith, which sat sprawled on the far bank of the river. He touched his black with his sunburst spurs and the horse broke into a trot.

But he suddenly drew rein when he saw the two men come tumbling out of the willows that were growing along the bank of the river. He sat his saddle watching as the pair, locked together like some bizarre puzzle, rolled over and over on the ground.

One of the men managed to disengage himself. He leaped to his feet and kicked the man on the ground, who then got to his feet and threw a right, which his opponent easily deflected by thrusting his forearm forward.

Cimarron watched the fight for a moment. He was about to move on when one of the men went for his gun.

"Hold it, you two," he shouted, and rode up to the men, who had been momentarily immoblized by his words.

"You two want to go at it knuckle and skull," he said when he drew rein beside them, "that's just fine with me. But there'll be no killing."

"This matter's private between Billy and me, mister," the taller and older of the two men shot back.

"You were going to gun me down, Charlie," Billy cried in an awed tone of voice as he stared fixedly at the gun in Charlie's hand. "And me, I'm not even armed."

"Gunning you down's too good for a bastard like you," Charlie countered. "What I ought to do is I ought to stake you out on the ground and cut your eyelids off so the sun can

9

blind you. A man who'd steal from his employer deserves no better."

"I didn't steal from you," Billy insisted, his voice rising.

"Cows you stole. Money of mine."

"I never stole a damned thing from you or your ranch."

"Put that gun away, Charlie," Cimarron ordered. "Before it goes off and you drill somebody."

"Mind your own business, mister," Charlie growled, his gun swiveling around to point in Cimarron's direction.

Without another word, Cimarron slid his right boot from its stirrup and kicked out. His boot struck Charlie's hand, and the gun, as Charlie's finger convulsed on its trigger, fired. Cimarron kicked out a second time and this time he knocked the gun from Charlie's hand.

Enraged, Charlie seized Cimarron's boot and pulled hard on it.

Cimarron made a grab for his saddle horn but missed it. A moment later, he hit the ground and a moment after that Charlie was kneeling on the ground straddling him, his fists pummeling both sides of Cimarron's head.

Cimarron brought one knee up and rammed it into Charlie's groin. As Charlie yelped in pain and clutched his genitals in both hands, Cimarron seized both of the man's wrists and, getting up on his knees, hurled him to one side.

Charlie's body struck a deadfall and he lay dazed for a moment before getting to his hands and knees and shaking his head groggily.

Cimarron heard the sound of splashing behind him and he turned to find Billy racing through the shallows of the river. When Billy came out of the river on the opposite bank, he kept on running without looking back.

Cimarron's knees buckled as he was suddenly struck on the shoulder from behind. He turned and saw the limb that had been broken from the deadfall in Charlie's hand. It was rising . . .

Cimarron unleathered his gun in one swift movement and fired, shattering the deadwood. He reached out before his

10

startled attacker could make another move and placed his gun against the base of the man's throat.

"I'm a deputy marshal and you, mister, are under arrest as of this minute," he announced. "Now put your hands on top of your head."

When Charlie had obeyed his order, Cimarron backed toward his black, and when he reached it, he fumbled about in his saddlebag, finally coming up with a pair of handcuffs. He bent down, picked up Charlie's gun, and placed it in his waistband.

"Now, then," he said stonily, "I'm going to put these cuffs on you and you're going to walk ahead of me to Fort Smith."

"I didn't shoot Billy," Charlie protested. "I was just trying to scare him." He smiled warily. "You can't put a man in jail for fistfighting like Billy and me were just doing."

"I can put you in jail for assault with a deadly weapon."

"I didn't draw on you," Charlie protested.

"That branch you broke off the deadfall is the deadly weapon I'm talking about, not your gun. You're under arrest like I just said for assault with a deadly weapon with the intent to kill or maim. That charge'll get you not less than one nor more than five years. At hard labor."

Cimarron moved toward Charlie, his gun leveled at his attacker's midsection, the handcuffs clinking in his left hand.

He halted when he heard the sound of hoofbeats behind him. Shifting position so he could keep Charlie under his gun and also see who was riding toward him, he stared uneasily at the six riders bearing down upon him.

Case Marlow was leading the pack. His three sons were right behind him. And behind them rode Jenny. Beside her rode a man who was wearing a black suit and carrying a black book.

Four Marlow six-guns were aimed at Cimarron.

"Throw down your iron," the elder Marlow barked as he drew rein in front of Cimarron.

Cimarron dropped his gun to the ground.

"Sooner," Case said to his youngest son, "go get his gun and then get around behind him."

As Sooner got out of the saddle, Charlie held up his hands and, waving them nervously in front of him, said, "Don't shoot! Please, don't none of you shoot!"

Case ignored him, and when Sooner had picked up Cimarron's .44 and jammed it into his cartridge belt, he motioned with his gun and Sooner stepped around behind Cimarron.

Cimarron felt the barrel of Sooner's gun pressing against his spine. "Case, what's this all about?" he inquired.

"Me," Jenny said cheerfully as she walked her horse up beside her father's. "Me and you, Cimarron."

Cimarron frowned. He hooked his thumbs in his cartridge belt and stood his ground, wondering, waiting.

"You're a trifling man, Cimarron," Case said, his lips barely moving.

"Our sister's paid—she's paying the price for your trifling with her," Bart Marlow snarled.

Jamie tilted his stetson back on his head with the barrel of his gun and said, "But we aim to set things right between the two of you."

"I don't have the least little notion of what it is you boys are talking about," Cimarron lied, trying for a smile but promptly losing it as Case Marlow's eyes blazed in anger.

"You know damned well what we're talking about," Sooner stated from behind Cimarron.

"I don't and that's a fact," Cimarron lied again.

"Show him what we're talking about, Jenny," Bart commanded, and Jenny obligingly got out of the saddle to stand beside her mare, both of her hands resting lightly on the bulge of her belly that hiked the front of her dress up to reveal her ankles.

"It's yours, Cimarron," she said sweetly, smiling brilliantly. "Ours, I mean. If it's a girl, I thought we could name her Dorothy. I just love that name—Dorothy. But if it's a boy, of course we'll name him Cimarron, Junior."

Cimarron, shaking his head in an effort to deny the reality of what he saw, said "You're—"

"She's pregnant!" Case shouted. "And you're the one that went and got her in a family way."

"You're going to do right by our sister," Sooner declared ominously, and his gun suddenly threatened to snap Cimarron's spine.

"You're going to marry her," Jamie declared gruffly.

"Where shall we go on our honeymoon, Cimarron?" Jenny asked. "Tulsey Town? Or all the way up to Dodge City?"

"I—you—we—" Cimarron gave it up and fell silent.

"Preacher," Case said, and beckoned to the man on the horse behind him. "Come along up here and let's get the ceremony over and done with."

As the preacher, his book in his hand, got out of the saddle, Jenny skipped up to Cimarron, took his arm, and stood with him, facing her father and two of her brothers.

"Wait a minute," Cimarron said suddenly. "Now, just hold on a minute. How the hell do you know I'm the daddy?"

"Jenny told us you were," Jamie replied as if that settled the matter.

"Maybe she's been with other men besides me," Cimarron pointed out.

"So you admit to what you did to her," Case roared, his face suddenly aflame.

"Cimarron, there never was anyone else," Jenny declared fervently, and squeezed his arm. "There was always only you."

"You can't railroad me into marriage," Cimarron protested, knowing full well that the Marlow clan could and, it looked like, would do just that. "I'm not fit to be the husband of such a fine woman as Jenny here. I'm never home. Hell, I haven't even got a place I can call home. I'm broke most of the time, and when I'm not, I—I get drunk! I gamble. I forni—" His lips snapped shut just in time.

"You're going to make an honest woman out of my daughter, Cimarron," Case said sternly. "When Jenny told us she'd spotted you riding through Parson's Point a while back, we got the preacher and rode right out after you. We've been trying for some time to get our hands on you, and now we have. You're going to marry Jenny because she has got to get herself married now that she's got herself in the fix you can plainly see she's in. Preacher, get a move on!''

The preacher, a solemn expression on his round face as he stood in front of Cimarron and the still-smiling Jenny, opened his black book. ''Dearly beloved—''

''I tell you, Case,'' Cimarron interrupted, ''I'd be hopeless as a husband. You just can't go and do a thing like that to Jenny—saddle her with me is what I mean. Now, if you'll just give this matter some serious thought, you'll see that. Why, this man standing next to me has a whole lot more character than I'll ever hope to have.''

An idea suddenly occurred to Cimarron, and desperate, he decided he had nothing to lose by trying what he had in mind. And if it worked he had a lot to gain. Namely, freedom.

''Charlie here,'' he said, ''owns a ranch. Cattle. He's not a wealthy man, but he makes do and gets by. He makes more money by far than I do in any given year, I'll wager. He could give Jenny a real good home. Couldn't you, Charlie?'' Cimarron jabbed Charlie in the ribs with his elbow.

''I'm not a marrying man,'' Charlie snapped. ''You got yourself into this, mister, you get yourself out of it.'' He snickered. ''In,'' he said knowingly. ''Out,'' he added, and burst into loud laughter.

''Case,'' Cimarron said soberly, ''just give me a minute to talk to my friend Charlie here. Will you do that, Case?''

As Case hesitated, Cimarron seized Charlie's arm. Leaning close to the man, he muttered, ''Not less than one year and not more than five years is what you'll get by the time Judge Parker's through with you. At hard labor! I'll make a deal with you, Charlie, old son. You marry Jenny and I'll forget all about charging you with assault with a deadly weapon with the intent to kill or maim me.''

Charlie remained silent.

Cimarron turned to face Case Marlow and said, "Charlie here would be right proud to marry Jenny, Case. He just told me he'd never laid even one of his eyes on such a comely woman before."

"Well," Case drawled, "I don't see that it matters all that much who she marries just so she does marry somebody so she'll be respectable when her time comes."

"No, Pa," Jenny shrieked. "I don't want Charlie, whoever he might be. I want Cimarron!"

"Shut your mouth, girl," Case bellowed. "You got no say in this. It's your damned waywardness that caused us this problem in the first place, so you'll marry whoever I tell you to marry."

"Pa, you just can't go and do this to me. Look at him." Jenny pointed to Charlie. "He's skinny as a snake. He's got arms like an ape."

"It's most likely you'll draw closer to five years than just one, Charlie," Cimarron muttered, jabbing Charlie in the ribs a second time. "Judge Parker's a harsh man. Some say a mean man. Think on all that hard labor you're going to have to endure—if you can endure it. Rack that up against you and Jenny living together in bedded—I mean, wedded bliss and there's just one conclusion you can jump to."

"No," Charlie yelled at the top of his voice.

"I'll lie and say you murdered Billy," Cimarron snarled in a vicious whisper. "I'll say I saw you rape a woman. You won't go to jail, Charlie, old son. What you'll do is hang."

"Yes," Charlie yelled at the top of his voice.

"No," Jenny cried, and threw her arms around Cimarron's neck. "It's you I want to marry, Cimarron."

Cimarron gently disengaged her arms and moved aside so that she was standing next to Charlie.

The preacher looked back over his shoulder at Case, and when Case nodded curtly, he turned to Charlie. "May I know your last name, sir? For purposes of the ceremony?"

"Lendell," Charlie said glumly.

"Hope you two have a real happy honeymoon," Cimarron

said. He handed Charlie the gun he had taken from him and pulled his own gun out of Sooner's belt and holstered it.

Jenny began to wail as Cimarron returned the handcuffs to his saddlebag and then swung into his saddle.

"Dearly beloved," intoned the preacher, his eyes on the words printed in the open book he held in his hands. "We are gathered here together to join this man and this woman . . ."

Cimarron raked the black with his spurs and went galloping across the river toward Fort Smith.

As he emerged from the river just north of Belle Point, a whistle shrieked, and he turned his head to see a round canvas tent standing on the bluff where the Poteau River joined the Arkansas.

He sat his saddle, marveling, as a man wearing black trousers, a black broadcloth coat, elastic-sided black shoes, a boiled white shirt, a black string tie, and a black top hat appeared from around the tent, a beribboned baton in his right hand. Stepping high, the man marched in an easterly direction, and a moment later a calliope mounted on a brightly painted wagon appeared to spill its steam and unique music into the air.

Behind the calliope marched two more men carrying a long banner that was stretched between them. It bore the words, white on black velvet: SIMPSON'S COLOSSAL CIRCUS AND MENAGERIE.

Next in line was a cavorting clown wearing a baggy white suit and a pie plate of a red hat, his face whitened and dotted with glittering spangles.

Cimarron watched as the procession lengthened to include two elephants, each of them ridden by young women with veils over the lower halves of their faces and filmy garments covering their bodies. Behind the elephants came wagons drawn by teams of horses, their sides decorated with carved and gilded female figures discreetly draped. Perched atop the band-wagon were five men wearing scarlet uniforms richly adorned with gold braid who began to play their brass instruments in competition with the man seated at the keyboard of the calliope.

Children appeared from everywhere to march beside the gaudy parade. Men and women lined the sidewalks, gaping and pointng, their mouths open in undisguised awe as cages bearing lions, a rhinoceros, and monkeys rolled by on sturdy wagons.

Behind the cages were four young men who went tumbling and cartwheeling down the street, leaping into the air to land on the shoulders of their companions—a blur of movement that caused the growing crowd first to gasp and then to break into appreciative applause.

Cimarron, when the last of the parade had finally passed him, fell in behind it. He rode down the street after it, past the cemetery, and then he turned left and headed for Rogers Avenue.

He turned left again at the intersection and then entered the stone-walled compound within which was the federal courthouse and the gallows.

As he passed the macabre platform, he nodded to George Maledon, the hangman, who stood nonchalantly on one of the several traps set in the floor as he carefully examined the noose that dangled from an I-beam. " 'Morning, George.''

"Nice day,'' Maledon responded, running his slender fingers almost lovingly along the hemp.

"For a hanging?''

"Just one this morning.''

"Who's the unlucky son of a bitch this time?''

"Ernie Wilcox.''

Cimarron felt a sinking sensation in the pit of his stomach as he sat his saddle staring at the noose in Maledon's hands. He felt queasy partly because he recalled all too well the time several years ago when he had nearly become a victim of the gallows and partly because he was sorry to hear that eighteen-year-old Ernie Wilcox was to be its next victim.

"The jury convicted Wilcox of murdering Labrette, did they?'' he asked, knowing it was a foolish question while vaguely wishing that Maledon would reply in the negative.

"They did, Cimarron. You can carve another notch in your

gun. You were the one who brought Wilcox in, weren't you?"

"I was the one. Well, have yourself a good day, George."

As Cimarron headed toward the courthouse, Maledon called out, "I always have a good day when I've a hanging to oversee."

A shudder passed through Cimarron's body. He had suddenly grown cold, although the sun still burned in the cloudless blue sky above him.

He dismounted, tethered his horse to the hitch rail in front of the courthouse, and then went inside and made his way to Marshal Upham's office.

Upham opened the door in response to Cimarron's knock and said, "Oh, it's you, is it? I was expecting someone else."

Cimarron followed Upham across the office after closing the door behind him and sat down in one of the two leather chairs facing the desk.

Upham, once he was seated behind his desk, began to shuffle papers. "I wasn't expecting to see you, Cimarron. I find it's a rare occasion when I have to welcome a bounty hunter to my office."

"Marshal, I'm not a bounty hunter."

"The last time you were in this office you declared yourself to be one. Maybe not in so many words. But—"

"I'll tell you what happened." Cimarron proceeded to do so, and he had just finished speaking when there was a tentative knock on the door.

Upham rose and crossed the office. He opened the door and said, "Ah, it's you Miss Powell. Come in, please."

Cimarron turned in his chair to watch Upham bow the young woman he had called Miss Powell into his office.

He took in her heart-shaped face, her slim figure and almost nonexistent waist. His eyes rose from her full hips to her equally full breasts and then to her very attractive face. Her eyes were blue. Her skin was rosy. Pert little nose she's got, he thought. Nice full lips, too.

"This deputy, Miss Powell, is named Cimarron," Upham declared.

Cimarron sprang to his feet and took the hand Miss Powell held out to him. He shook it, finding her grip surprisingly strong. "I'm pleased to make your acquaintance, Miss Powell."

"You look exactly the way a deputy marshal should look, Cimarron," Miss Powell said in her slightly husky voice after giving him an appraising look. "So self-confident and—virile." She sat down in the empty chair beside Cimarron's and turned to face Upham, who had seated himself behind his desk. "I hope I didn't interrupt anything, Marshal."

"Not at all, not at all. And if you had—why, I must say that an interruption by such a lovely young woman as yourself would be nothing but most welcome."

"What a charming man you are, Marshal." Turning to Cimarron, who was seated again, Miss Powell asked, "Isn't he charming, Cimarron?"

"Well—" Cimarron caught the glare Upham was giving him. "Oh, he's charming, all right. Never met a more charming man than the marshal."

Upham's glare faded and was replaced by a beatific, almost idiotic smile as he turned his attention to Miss Powell. "Judge Parker told me before he left town yesterday that you would be here to see me this morning. He also asked me to do whatever I could to help you. What can I do to help you, Miss Powell?"

"Judge Parker was more than kind to me when we met yesterday. He said he felt sure that you would see your way clear to provide our circus with the protection we shall most sorely need as we journey west through Indian Territory on our way to California."

"Protection?" Upham regarded his visitor quizzically.

"We've all heard how perfectly dreadful conditions are in the Territory, Marshal, so we petitioned Judge Parker to help us. He said it was your province to provide protection and he didn't want to interfere with the operation of your office. He referred me to you. I hoped that you would provide us with a—is it called a posse?''

"Is what called a posse?'' Upham asked, obviously puzzled.

"I'm talking about an armed guard to escort Simpson's Colossal Circus through the Territory,'' Miss Powell explained. "A dozen or so men should do quite nicely.''

"A dozen or so men—'' Upham fell back in his chair.

"You ought to be able to manage that easy, Marshal,'' Cimarron commented. "A dozen of your deputies ought to be able to keep all those wild animals in their cages and all those wild Indians who're roaming around in the Territory out of the circus tent.''

"That's enough, Cimarron,'' Upham snapped angrily. And then he began to smile. A moment later, he was beaming. "All of my deputies, Miss Powell, are at present on the scout in the Territory.'' He cleared his throat. "All but one, that is.''

"Now, wait just one damned minute, Marshal,'' Cimarron almost shouted, half-rising from his chair. Upham scowled at him and he sat back down.

"Cimarron, I'm sure,'' Upham said to Miss Powell, "will be happy to escort you and the other people in the circus until you reach northern Texas.''

"I'm not riding shotgun for any circus,'' Cimarron declared hotly.

Miss Powell gave him a disappointed look.

Upham gave him another fierce scowl. "Now that you've got bounty hunting out of your system, Cimarron, I assumed—I hope not mistakenly—that you were ready to accept another assignment from the court.''

"I am ready. I want another assignment, but—''

"I've just given you one. You will guide Simpson's Circus across the Territory. You will be responsible for the safety of its people and its property. As an officer of this court, you will uphold the fine reputation its deputy marshals have earned and carry on in their tradition of selfless service in the protection of the lives and property of innocent people in the Indian Territory."

"You will help us, then, Cimarron?" Miss Powell inquired tentatively. She leaned toward him and Cimarron found himself staring down at the provocative cleavage her square-necked gown revealed.

"I will," he was surprised to hear himself say.

"Oh, I'm so glad!" Miss Powell exclaimed, reaching out and squeezing his hand. "I'm sure I'll be safe in your strong and capable hands, Cimarron."

"I'm not so sure you will be," Upham muttered in a barely audible voice, his eyes on Cimarron, whose eyes were still on Miss Powell's cleavage.

"We all will be," Miss Powell added, and then, "did you just say something, Marshal?"

"Nothing of any import."

"Well, I'd better be getting back to the lot," Miss Powell announced, rising from her chair.

"You might as well go right along with her, Cimarron," Upham suggested. He stood up and rounded his desk. Taking Miss Powell's arm, he led her to the door, where he bowed and kissed the hand she extended to him.

"Thank you ever so much for your cooperation, Marshal," she said. "And do be sure to thank Judge Parker as well."

Cimarron ignored the sly wink Upham gave him as Miss Powell left the office. He followed her out of the room and later, as they came out into the compound, he freed his horse and began to lead it toward the gate.

"Whatever in the world are all these people doing here?" Miss Powell asked him as more and more people streamed through the gate to join those already gathered in front of the gallows platform.

"They've come for the hanging," Cimarron answered.

"Hanging?"

Cimarron pointed to the noose dangling in the air.

"Oh, how dreadful!"

"When do you circus people perform?"

21

"At night. Why?"

"Well, it's a good thing it's not in the morning. You'd sell few tickets if you performed this morning. Everybody'd come instead to see the circus that's about to take place here."

"Circus? I'm afraid I don't understand."

"People do seem to enjoy hangings. They come from miles around to see one. It's them that turn the proceedings into a circus of sorts." Cimarron pointed.

Miss Powell gazed at the family group that was noisily picnicking near the stone wall. "You westerners must have a terribly warped idea of what constitutes entertainment."

"We westerners aren't much different at bottom from easterners or northerners or southerners, I reckon. Most people dote on death—somebody else's. That's why a lot of them go to the circus."

"I don't follow you."

"They may not know it, but a bunch of them're hoping to see a trapeze artist fall to his death. Or a lion tear his tamer to pieces."

"Is that the man they're going to hang?"

Cimarron glanced in the direction Miss Powell was looking and saw Ernie Wilcox being marched from the jail, which was in the basement of the courthouse. Preceding him was a preacher. Following him were two armed jail attendants.

"That's the man."

"Hurry. Let's get out of here. I don't want to witness what's going to happen."

Me neither, Cimarron thought as he followed Miss Powell through the gate.

"The circus lot is on the bluff by the river," Miss Powell informed him. "We'll be there in no time."

"What is it exactly that you do in the circus, Miss Powell?"

"Call me Lucinda, Cimarron. I'm sure we're going to become the very best of friends during our upcoming journey together. To answer your question, I'm what circus people sometimes call a high rider."

"What's that?"

22

"I ride a Lipizzaner stallion, which I control by using only my wrists, calves, and by subtly shifting my body's weight. The method is called high-school riding or, in French, *haute école*. One can make the Lipizzaner—one that has been high-school-trained—do all sorts of things: trot, waltz, sidestep, pirouette, and much more. Have you ever seen a high rider perform, Cimarron?"

But Cimarron was no longer paying attention to Lucinda. He was staring, a frown on his face, at the woman who was standing across the street from the compound gate, her arms at her sides, a forlorn expression on her face.

"Lucinda," he said, "you go on along to the circus lot. There's somebody over there I've got to have a word with. I'll catch up with you later."

He led his black across the street and stopped in front of Esther Lane. She didn't look up at him as she continued to stare into the compound.

"Miss Lane," he said softly, "you oughtn't to be here." When she did not respond, he gently touched her arm.

She looked up at him. "Cimarron."

"I'll take you someplace where you won't have to see—"

"I hope you're happy now," she said, her voice colorless. "You brought Ernie to jail and now he's going to—they're going to hang him!" She began to weep, her hands covering her face.

"It's not my doing," Cimarron argued. "He had himself a trial and was convicted of murder."

"I know that," Esther cried, uncovering her tear-stained face. "I was at the trial. I hired a lawyer to defend Ernie, but the man—all he could do was—he couldn't do anything. Not in the face of all those eyewitnesses who testified they saw Ernie kill Mr. Labrette."

Cimarron turned and stared through the compound gate at the noose resting loosely—but not for long, he thought—around Wilcox's neck as the preacher read unheard words from his Bible.

"Everyone was against Ernie right from the start," Esther

continued, fighting back her tears. "The people in McAlester, the newspaper there. They wrote in the paper that it was men like Ernie who had to be rooted out—that's what they wrote, 'rooted out'—and hanged before the Territory could ever hope to become a place for decent people to live.

"They wrote that guns in the hands of men like Ernie were lethal and that the forty-five-caliber bullet that took Mr. Labrette's life was a symbol of the evil of men like my poor Ernie. They—"

Cimarron spun around to face Esther. "Did you just say a forty-five-caliber bullet?"

She nodded dumbly, her tears beginning again.

Cimarron's thoughts raced. He recalled apprehending Wilcox in Esther's bedroom that dark night. He remembered the gun he had taken away from Wilcox.

"That gun I took from Wilcox, was it the only one he owned?"

"Yes. He wanted to buy a better—a newer one—but he never had enough money at any one time."

An image of Wilcox's Model 1849 .31-caliber revolver flashed in Cimarron's mind. He saw it clearly—its five-inch octagon barrel, its five-chambered cylinder, its blue finish.

He leaped aboard his black and went galloping across the street and into the compound, where he circled the boisterous crowd until he reached the steps at the side of the gallows platform. He let out a whoop, and when the two jail attendants guarding Wilcox turned toward him, their guns in their hands, he yelled, "Stop the hanging!"

"Cimarron," the attendant nearest him responded, "what the hell are you talking about?"

"George," Cimarron yelled, gesturing wildly, "get that noose off Wilcox's neck."

Maledon merely stared at Cimarron in surprise as the preacher spluttered and twitched nervously.

"Do it, George," Cimarron shouted. "Stop the hanging!"

The other jail attendant shook his head and said, "Only Judge Parker can stop a hanging, Cimarron. You know that."

"And the judge is out of town," his companion told Cimarron. "He's giving a speech over in Van Buren."

Cimarron swore and said, "All I'm asking you to do is postpone the hanging. When Judge Parker gets back to town, I'll talk to him. I'll take the responsibility for delaying the hanging."

"No, sir, Cimarron," Maledon said firmly. "We're going ahead with this. You must have gone crazy or something. Stop the hanging, he says. Nobody stops one of George Maledon's hangings. Judge Parker never even did."

The words had a galvanizing effect on Cimarron. He leaped from the saddle, but as he bounded up the steps, both jail attendants aimed their six-guns at him and he halted halfway to the platform.

"We'll shoot you if we have to," one of them said.

"If you force us to," the other one said.

Cimarron held out his hands in a helpless gesture. "You've got me dead to rights, boys. But let's us talk this thing over like the reasonable men we are." He climbed up onto the platform.

The jail attendants both took a step backward.

Cimarron suddenly reached out and seized the preacher. Using the man as a shield, he edged around the attendants and then reached out with his free hand and removed the noose from around Wilcox's neck.

"Cimarron," Wilcox exclaimed. "I never in my life thought I'd be glad to see you again."

"Get down from here and up behind the cantle of my saddle, Wilcox."

Wilcox fled from the platform, and when he was on Cimarron's black, Cimarron drew his .44. "You two," he said to the attendants, "drop your guns. On the trap."

When they had done so, Cimarron said, "George, you go down and around back and pull your little lever."

Moments later, as the crowd stared in shocked silence at the four men remaining on the platform, Maledon sprung the trap and the two revolvers fell through it to the ground below.

A man in the watching crowd suddenly fired at Cimarron.

He spun around as the bullet zipped past him, the preacher still held in front of him and obviously terrified, and fired a shot over the heads of the people in the crowd.

As women screamed and a baby began to bellow, he yelled, "I've got me five shots left. Now, who else wants to try to be a hero?"

No one answered him.

The crowd began to shrink away from the gallows. Then, as if responding to some unseen signal, people began running for the gate of the compound. Some of them fell to the ground in their haste only to be trampled by the frantic people behind them.

Cimarron released the preacher and leaped from the platform as Marshal Upham's head appeared in his open office window. Once he was in the saddle, he turned his black and galloped toward the low stone wall of the compound because the gate was blocked by the fleeing throng.

"*Cimarron!*"

Cimarron didn't look back at the sound of his name, which had been shouted at the top of Marshal Upham's voice.

"Just what the hell do you think you're doing?" Upham roared as Cimarron's black leaped over a partially crumbled portion of the stone wall and went galloping toward the river.

"Where are we going?" Wilcox asked breathlessly.

There was a grin on Cimarron's face as he replied, "You and me, Wilcox, we're running away to join the circus."

2

Cimarron's grin faded and then vanished completely as he holstered his revolver and rode out of Fort Smith, heading south.

His lips were a thin line above his square jaw and below his wide-nostriled nose, and his eyes, as green and piercing as pine needles, were cold but not lifeless. They gleamed as he glanced back over his shoulder for signs of pursuit. They glowed as he thought of what he had just done and then they darkened as he wondered if he had done the right thing.

The thin line of his lips grew even thinner and muscles twitched slightly in his sunken cheeks beneath his prominent cheekbones.

His straight black hair, which ranged down over his ears and the nape of his neck, flew in the wind, and the brim of his flat-topped black stetson snapped in it. Sweat began to bead on his broad and deeply creased forehead. He sat straight but not stiffly in the saddle, his callused hands tight on the reins. His slender, almost bony body, a mass of taut muscle, bent forward over his saddle horn as he spurred his horse.

With his dusty black boots, into which his worn and faded jeans were tucked, planted firmly in his stirrups and sticking out almost at right angles to his black's body, he rode on, unmindful of the way his blue bandanna, flicked by the wind, fluttered against his face from time to time, or of the fact that the sweat gathering on his thick chest, broad back, and brawny shoulders was causing his shirt to stick to his skin.

The scar on his face, which began just below his left eye and curved down across his cheekbone to end just above the corner of his mouth, was almost white against the sun-bronzed skin of the rest of his face.

Each of the loops on his black-leather gun belt was occupied by a cartridge. The holster that hung from the belt, which slapped against his thigh as he rode on, housed his single-action Frontier Colt .44 from which he had cut away the trigger guard. Behind him, the stock of his Winchester '73 protruded from its saddle scabbard, and the hilt of a bowie knife was barely visible above the top of his right boot.

As he and Wilcox galloped onto the circus lot on the bluff above the Poteau River, an elephant emerged from behind the circular canvas circus tent, and when the black under the two men saw and smelled the animal, it reared, its front legs wildly pawing the air.

"Hell fire and damnation!" Cimarron shouted as he fought for control of his mount. Behind him, Wilcox seized his shoulders to keep from falling from the saddle.

"Get that beast out of here," Cimarron yelled at the man who was sitting placidly on the elephant's neck, his legs draped down behind the animal's idly flapping ears.

The man Cimarron had addressed prodded the elephant with the bull hook he held in his right hand, and the elephant, its small eyes blinking and its big ears still flapping, lumbered across the lot and out of sight behind a smaller tent.

Lucinda Powell emerged from a wagon standing next to the small tent. She ran up to the black, grabbed its bridle, and yanked hard on it, bringing the black's feet down to the ground, where they remained as she spoke to the horse—her words so softly whispered that Cimarron heard none of them.

Wilcox, obeying Cimarron's muttered command, slid out of the saddle and stood staring wide-eyed at Lucinda, who released her hold on the bridle and looked up at Cimarron.

"Horses," she said, "other than circus horses, that is, tend to become frightened of elephants."

"Is that a fact?" Cimarron grumbled as he got out of the saddle. "Now, were you to tell me that there's the sun sitting up there in the sky, I'd believe you even if you were telling me what I already know, just like you just did about my horse and your elephant."

Lucinda smiled faintly. "There really is no need for you to be upset because I quieted your horse, Cimarron. I was only trying to help."

"I'm obliged to you."

Lucinda, in response to the surliness with which Cimarron had thanked her, merely smiled more broadly and said, "I happen to know a great deal about horses, having worked with my Lipizzaner for years, but that doesn't make me any less of a woman or you any less of a man because I happened to be the one who gentled your mount."

"There's no way in the world you could make *him* less of a man," declared an enormously fat woman as she came up to the trio standing beside Cimarron's horse. "Not unless you were to take a knife and geld him, there isn't." Her shrill, decidedly girlish laughter erupted from her thick throat, and as it did so, her body, which was laden with thick folds of flesh, shook and bounced and billowed. "He's one hundred percent he-man," the woman continued when her laughter ended. "Maybe one hundred and *ten* percent. You can tell that just by looking at him."

Cimarron, despite his annoyance at Lucinda, which he knew was caused by embarrassment resulting from his failure to curb his horse before she had done so, grinned at the fat woman and touched the brim of his hat to her. "I haven't had such a fine compliment from a lady in—well, ever, come to think on it."

"I'm Babe Folsom," the woman announced in a voice that was as thin as her body was fat. "See? That's my name and picture up there on the banner line." She pointed, her brown

29

eyes dancing, and then proudly patted her short blond hair, which was a gleaming helmet of ringlets.

Cimarron stared at the gaudily painted canvas panel that hung among several others above the entrance to the smaller tent that stood not far from the main one. "Babe Folsom," he read aloud. "The Fattest Woman in the World."

"And the lustiest one too," Babe added, and began to giggle again.

"Babe!" Lucinda cried, her face flushing. "Shame on you!"

"Oh, don't be such a prude, Lucinda," Babe chided without anger. "You sound like you'd been weaned on prunes and proverbs. Why shouldn't I speak the truth, especially when I'm talking about myself? Who gets hurt? Nobody, that's who." She reached out, and her pudgy fingers patted Cimarron's cheek. "I can't keep count—I lost count long ago—of all the men who have climbed this mountain that's me!" She put one huge arm around Cimarron's waist. "What's your name, sweetheart?"

"Cimarron."

"He's a deputy marshal," Lucinda told Babe. "He's going to escort us all safely through Indian Territory."

The fleshy folds of Babe's face wiggled as she shook her head from side to side. "Lucinda, you listen to me. Maybe he'll escort our men safely through the Territory, but us women—well, that may turn out to be another matter entirely. A man like him—I know the type. Look at those evil green eyes of his! I'd say they're the eyes of a man who can be wicked where women are concerned."

"Please pay her no mind, Cimarron," Lucinda advised, her eyes averted.

Cimarron, grinning again, said, "I reckon she's gone and read my brand right."

"Of course I have," Babe hooted happily, slapping her enormous hips with both hands. "I can read men as easy as I read books. Easier even."

"Since you admit that Babe is right in her judgment of

you," Lucinda said to Cimarron, "I shall have to be wary of you, shan't I?"

Cimarron said nothing, but he continued to grin.

"That's my wagon over there," Babe declared, pointing to it. "Cimarron, you come by and we'll get drunk together sometime. How about tonight after the show?"

"I thank you kindly for the invitation, Babe. I might just do that."

"Might," Babe repeated, and assumed a doleful look of melodramatic sorrow. "That's a far piece from a promise," she said as she blew a kiss to Cimarron and waddled away.

"Lucinda," Cimarron said, "this here's Ernie Wilcox."

"How do you do, Ernie?"

"I'm real pleased to meet you, Miss—"

"Lucinda."

"—Lucinda. Real pleased." Ernie stretched out a hand and then blushed as Lucinda leaned toward him. After glancing nervously at Cimarron, he lightly brushed her smooth cheek with his lips.

"If you gentlemen like, I shall be happy to show you around the lot and introduce you to some of our people."

"Let's do that," Cimarron said. "But let's do it fairly fast and without causing any fuss on account of I've—me and Ernie've got to light out of here real quick before some lawman comes looking for us."

"You're expecting trouble with the law?" Lucinda asked uneasily. "I thought Marshal Upham said you were a deputy marshal."

"He did and I am, but it's a long story and I'll tell it all to you sometime when you and me've got nothing better to do than talk." His grin faltered on the edge of a leer. He tethered his horse to a tent stake and then, with Lucinda leading the way, walked with Wilcox across the circus lot.

"Those are the butchers," she remarked, indicating the men setting up concession stands. "Those men, they're roustabouts," she said, indicating the men checking the stakes and ropes that held the circus and sideshow tents in place. "Here we are."

She knocked on the door of a wagon, and when it opened a moment later, she said, "Hello, Mr. Simpson. This gentleman" —she nodded in Cimarron's direction—"is the deputy marshal I mentioned to you."

The gray-haired man with the lined face and tired eyes said, "Cimarron, isn't it?"

Cimarron nodded and shook Simpson's hand.

"Mr. Simpson's our gaffer," Lucinda said. "Circus manager," she explained when she saw the puzzled look on Cimarron's face. "He also owns the show."

"Which is a way of saying," Simpson remarked, "that I own a headache and a half. Let me tell you, Cimarron, there are easier ways of earning a living than as a gaffer. A gaffer has to deal with temperamental performers—both people and beasts—pray the weather holds and the lot loafers can be persuaded to part with their money."

"Don't let Mr. Simpson fool you, Cimarron," Lucinda said, smiling. "He's been kicking sawdust longer than I've been alive and he loves it. Don't you, Mr. Simpson?"

Simpson nodded. "I do. Ever since my days as a funambulist—rope walker to you, Cimarron—I've been with one circus or another in one capacity or another. I just don't know how to live any other kind of life."

"Oh, there's Gunther and Ramona," Lucinda said. "Excuse us, Mr. Simpson, won't you?"

"Glad to have you with us, Cimarron," Simpson said. "I hear Indian Territory can be a dangerous place."

"It can be," Cimarron agreed.

"But Cimarron will see us safely through it," Lucinda assured Simpson, and then, surprising Cimarron, she took his arm and led him over to where a well-built blue-eyed blond man was standing talking to a slender but equally well-built raven-haired beauty who was almost as tall as her companion.

"Gunther von Kleist," Lucinda said when they reached the pair. "Gunther, this is Cimarron, a deputy marshal who will be traveling with us until we reach the Texas border. This is Ramona Bertolini, Cimarron.''

"I am very pleased to meet you," Gunther said, and when he took Cimarron's hand to shake it, Cimarron winced as a result of the man's iron grip.

"Same here," Cimarron said, his eyes on Ramona.

"Gunther," Lucinda said, "is our animal trainer and star attraction. He works in the arena with his lions and leopards and is really quite impressive. You'll see."

"And I," said Ramona, "am not a star attraction, I suppose?"

Her question had been directed to—flung at—Lucinda, who responded by saying, "Ramona is our funambulist."

"I never before met a lion tamer or a lady who can walk a rope way up in the middle of the air," Cimarron said. "I'm sure looking forward to seeing you two strut your stuff."

"But it is Lucinda who is the true star of the show," Gunther declared, gazing at Lucinda as Ramona watched him through narrowed eyes. "What she does—well, you will see, Cimarron, and when you do, you will not believe. The woman is a wizard with her Lipizzaner."

Cimarron nodded, watching Gunther watching Lucinda, his eyes filled with longing and, Cimarron decided, no little bit of lust. The man's voice was deep, resonant, and heavily accented. It was studded with harsh Germanic sounds so that words like "and" sounded like "und" and the letter "s" emerged from his lips sounding like "z." "Woman" became "voman." "Wizard" and "with" became "vizard" and "vith."

"Gunther," Ramona said, taking the man's arm, "let's go, shall we?"

"I have work to do," Gunther said, his eyes on Lucinda. "One of my leopards cut his paw this morning. I must go into town to the drugstore for some tincture of nicotine I can use to put him to sleep long enough for me to treat his wound."

"I'll go with you," Ramona volunteered, and led Gunther away.

"Ramona," Lucinda remarked idly as she, Cimarron, and

Wilcox continued their journey across the lot, "is in love with Gunther."

"Who's Gunther in love with?" Cimarron inquired.

"How should I know?"

"You know, I reckon. You couldn't miss those longing looks he was giving you. But I guess I'd best be about minding my own business."

"I suppose Gunther is fond of me, in a way. The eternal triangle." Lucinda sighed. "It does so complicate things."

Gunther's got lions and leopards in his arena, Cimarron thought, but I wonder if he knows he's got what I consider to be a couple of wildcats outside his arena; the wildcats could stand some taming, from the looks of the two of them.

"This is what we call the back yard," Lucinda said as they emerged in an open area behind the main tent. "Those two men over there—the one on the left, that's Matt Ledman, and the man with him is Tinker Sloan. They're both clowns."

Cimarron glanced at them. Ledman's face was lean and his features sharp. He towered above the short Sloan, who was flabbily built with a paunch that hung down over his belt. Ledman's face seemed frozen in a scowl, but Tinker's was blissfully smiling. Ledman's black hair was thick and straight. Tinker's blond and curly beneath his derby hat, which he wore at a rakish angle.

"Those two are as different as night and day," Cimarron commented.

"But both of them," Lucinda said, "can make an audience laugh."

Sloan turned, saw Lucinda, waved to her, and called her name before hurrying over to her.

Lucinda, turning to Cimarron, said, "I'd like you to meet Tinker Sloan, a man who could make even the Sphinx laugh."

"Or at least smile," Tinker said as he shook hands with Cimarron. "You're him, I bet."

"I'm who?"

"The gaffer told me to find you. He said you were on the lot. Said you were a big man. Said you had a gun in a hip

34

holster. 'Look for Lucinda,' he said. 'And if there's a big-booted, broad-shouldered, mean-eyed man with her, that's him,' he said.''

"Tinker, this is—" Lucinda began.

"I know who he is," Tinker interrupted. "He's Cimarron. The gaffer told me his name. How'd you get your name, Cimarron?"

"It more or less got me. Someone called me that once a ways back and it just sort of stuck to me like trail dust to a sweaty cowhand."

"It's a good name for a gunslinger," Tinker declared.

"I'm no gunslinger."

"You never killed a man?" Tinker prodded, disbelief causing his smooth brow to furrow.

"Yes, I have, but—"

"Aha! I spotted you for a gunslinger the minute I laid eyes on you. You walk wary. You keep shifting your eyes."

"Cimarron," Lucinda said to Tinker, "is a lawman. He's a deputy marshal who works for the court here in town."

"How many?" Tinker asked Cimarron.

"How many what?"

"Men did you kill?"

"I couldn't say for sure."

"A lot, I bet." There was an echo of awe in Tinker's voice.

"Tinker—you mind if I call you that?"

"It's fine with me."

"Well, Tinker," Cimarron continued, "you said that Mr. Simpson sent you to find me. You mind telling me what for?"

"Oh, I almost forgot. There's a girl. The candy butcher found her wandering around the lot looking lost, he told Mr. Simpson she was looking for you."

"A girl? Looking for me?"

"Actually, she wasn't looking for you. Not just for you, I mean. She was looking for him too." Tinker looked up at Wilcox. "If his name is Ernie Wilcox, she was."

35

"But I don't know any girls in town who'd be looking for me," Wilcox declared.

"Her name," Tinker said, "is Esther Lane."

"Esther!" Wilcox exclaimed. "She's here in Fort Smith?"

"Waiting by the ticket wagon for you."

"I'll show you where it is," Lucinda volunteered. "It's this way."

Cimarron and Wilcox left Tinker and followed her.

"Cimarron, did you hear?" Wilcox asked. "Esther's right here in town."

"I heard. I didn't have time to tell you about her. I had a talk with her just before they marched you out of jail back there in the compound."

"This man was in jail?" Lucinda asked, shrinking away from Wilcox.

"I told you before that it was a long story, Lucinda," Cimarron said. "I'll try to turn it into a short one. Yes, he was in jail. For a crime he didn't commit."

"I told you I never shot Labrette," Wilcox cried. "How come all of a sudden you believe me, Cimarron?"

"Has to do with something Esther said when we had our little talk. There she is."

Wilcox went running toward the spot opposite the sideshow tent where Esther stood, glancing first one way, then the other, her hands clasped tightly in front of her.

When he came up behind her, she cried out in alarm as he threw his arms around her.

"Are you sure he's an innocent man?" Lucinda asked Cimarron.

"I'm next to certain he is," Cimarron answered.

"But what if you're wrong? He said something about a shooting."

"Don't you fret about Wilcox, Lucinda. I'll be taking him off your hands most any minute now."

"Oh, Cimarron," Esther cried joyfully as he and Lucinda came up to her and Wilcox. She quickly disengaged herself from Wilcox's embrace and threw her arms around Cimarron's neck. She kissed him on the left cheek and then hugged him hard. "I'm ever so grateful to you for what you did for Ernie. I saw it all from outside the compound and followed you here on foot. I was so afraid you'd be hurt—shot—you or Ernie, perhaps both of you." She kissed him on the right cheek and hugged him even harder before releasing him.

"Well, now," Cimarron said, grinning, "what you just went and did makes what I went and did a while back more than just a little bit worthwhile."

Esther, flustered, looked down at the ground.

Wilcox glared at Cimarron for a moment and then smiled. "Keep that up, Esther, and you'll make a jealous man out of me."

"I'm sorry, Ernie," Esther murmured.

"I'm not," Cimarron said, and gave the pair a wink. Then, sobering, he looked around the lot at the townspeople beginning to crowd it and said, "The three of us have got to get ourselves out of here. Out of Fort Smith, too."

"We'll take my wagon," Esther said. "I left it at the livery in town when I arrived this morning."

"Good idea," Cimarron said thoughtfully. "You and Ernie can ride in the wagon. I'll ride alongside."

"But, Cimarron, you've been assigned to guard the circus," Lucinda protested. "If you leave us—"

"Hold on," Cimarron interrupted, holding up a hand. "I'm not deserting you and your people. Not for long, I'm not. Tell me something. Where were you folks planning on putting on your show next?"

"Step right up, folks!" bawled the sideshow barker from his platform, drowning out Lucinda's answer to Cimarron's question.

He cupped a hand behind his ear and Lucinda repeated, "We had no plans to play in Indian Territory."

"There's a town name of McAlester west of here," Cimarron said, and told her where it was and how to find it. "You get Mr. Simpson to take the show there. You can do that, can you?" he asked Lucinda.

"I think so. Yes, I'm sure I can. He'll welcome the chance to earn some money on our journey across the Territory."

"Good. I'll join up with you there. When are you pulling up stakes here?"

"After tonight's performance."

"It'll take you two, maybe three days to reach McAlester. I don't think you'll have too much trouble in Choctaw Nation. The Choctaws are a civilized people, though there are hard cases roaming around the Nation, so keep your men on the alert."

"They can handle themselves in a clem," Lucinda declared firmly.

"A clem?"

"That's what we call a fight, Cimarron. The minute somebody yells 'Hey, Rube,' all our men come running."

"Keep your eyes peeled for any Choctaw Lighthorsemen you might happen to run into. They're the Indian police. They'll help you, should you need help. So will any deputies like me you might run into. Now, you do like I said. Head west. Follow the Arkansas River, keep it on your right. When you hit the tracks of the Katy Railroad, follow them south until you come to McAlester."

"We'll probably need a license to play the town," Lucinda mused. "But I'm sure we can get one once we arrive there—if it's not too expensive."

"What do you usually pay for a license in the towns you hit?"

"Anywhere up to fifty dollars, but some towns try to put the squeeze on us and charge more even if there aren't enough people in the town to make it a paying proposition for us to put up even the sideshow tent or the one for the menagerie."

"If I have a chance, I'll try to get you a license, and if I do, Mr. Simpson can pay me back for what it cost. You think he'd do that?"

Lucinda nodded. "I'm sure he'd appreciate your help. If

you can get the license for us, it will save us some time once we arrive in McAlester.''

"Cimarron."

"Yes, Miss Lane?"

"Please. Call me Esther. I was wondering—do you think it's safe for Ernie to go back to McAlester? Isn't it likely that they'll send someone there after him?"

"It's likely," Cimarron agreed.

"Then we won't go back to McAlester, Ernie and I," Esther declared.

"You will go back," Cimarron contradicted.

Esther's face darkened.

"You'll go back," Cimarron continued, "on account of McAlester's the one place where we might be able to prove that Ernie didn't shoot Labrette. The one place where we might be able to figure out who it was who did shoot him."

"How are we going to do that, Cimarron?" Ernie asked.

"That's a good question. One I don't yet have the answer to. But the three of us, we ought to be able to come up with something. Hopefully sooner rather than later, once we get there."

"See the man who eats fire for breakfast, dinner, and supper," cried the sideshow barker. "See the lady who charms snakes."

"Miss Lane—I mean, Esther," Cimarron said, "you'd best head for the livery. Ernie and I'll be along presently."

"Inside you'll see marvels to rival the Seven Wonders of the World, ladies and gents," the barker shouted, waving both arms. "Why, even Johnny Tin Plate, who is heading our way right this very minute, has never seen the likes of what we have to offer inside, I'm more than willing to wager."

"Cimarron." Lucinda anxiously clutched his arm. "If you're trying to avoid the law, you had better get out of here fast."

"Why?"

"You heard the barker just now? You heard him mention Johnny Tin Plate?"

"I did."

"That's our name for the law. Look!"

Cimarron looked in the direction Lucinda had pointed and saw the deputy marshal walking across the lot toward the sideshow, his eyes roving, his right hand on his holstered revolver.

"He's come for me," Wilcox exclaimed. "Cimarron, what am I going to do?"

"His name's McMurty," Cimarron said. "And he's got two other guns with him—right behind him—Maxwell and Pettit." Cimarron turned to Lucinda, simultaneously pulling his hat down low on his forehead and turning his back to the deputies in the distance. "You go talk to those deputies," he ordered. "Keep them busy. They're hunting Ernie and me, and neither one of us wants to be found."

Lucinda, without a word, released her hold on Cimarron's arm and went running cross the lot. When she reached McMurty, she took his hand and shook it vigorously while managing to move the man around so that his back was to Cimarron, Wilcox, and Esther.

"Your horse," Wilcox said to Cimarron. "It's way over there and those three lawmen are between us and it. We'll never make it."

"Esther," Cimarron said, "you head for the livery stable."

"What are you and Ernie going to do?"

Cimarron gave her a shove instead of an answer and she hurried away.

"When you were a boy," Cimarron said to Wilcox, shouldering him toward the tent that housed the menagerie, "did you ever go to the circus?"

"Yes, but what—"

"Did you pay to get in?"

"No, I—" Wilcox stopped speaking, his face breaking into a sudden smile.

"Neither did I," Cimarron said. "Let's move!"

Both men dropped down to the ground. Cimarron raised the

canvas tent flap and they scuttled under it and then stood up to find themselves flanked by caged lions and leopards.

"Come on, Ernie!"

Both men ran across the tanbark- and straw-littered ground, past picketed horses and two staked elephants. When they reached the far side of the tent, they once again got down on their knees and crawled under the canvas and out into the open.

Cimarron glanced over his shoulder to find that Lucinda was leading the three deputies into the sideshow tent, smiling broadly as she waved away the efforts of the barker to sell the lawmen admission tickets.

When Cimarron reached his horse, he untethered it, leaped into the saddle, and then held out a hand to help Wilcox get up behind him.

Once Wilcox was aboard the black, Cimarron heeled the horse and rode around the menagerie tent, which effectively blocked him from the deputies, should they manage to escape from Lucinda and leave the sideshow tent.

As they galloped northeast across the bluff toward Fort Smith, Cimarron said, "Now comes the tricky part. Everybody in town's sure to know what happened, and if they see us, they'll like as not sound the alarm."

"What can we do?"

"Keep our hopes high and our heads low is all, I reckon."

Cimarron, when they reached the town, galloped past the waterfront saloons and brothels and then turned the black to the right and headed east until he came to a lightly populated area where he again turned the black to the right and rode south until he reached the rear of the livery stable.

Peering down the narrow passage that separated the livery from the building next to it, he was silent. But he called Esther's name when he saw her begin to cross the empty space between the two buildings several minutes later. He stood up in his stirrups and beckoned to her.

She came running down the alleyway.

"Esther," he said as she came breathlessly up to him, "get your wagon and drive it around back here."

Esther turned and ran back down the alleyway.

Cimarron restlessly sat his saddle as the minutes passed, silently urging Esther to hurry.

When her wagon finally came clattering around the side of the livery, Cimarron took off his hat and clapped it solidly down on Wilcox's head.

"Get down, Ernie, and then get up into that wagon," he ordered. "Keep my hat down low on your forehead so nobody'll recognize you—at least not easy."

"But they'll recognize you," Wilcox protested.

"That pair of horses pulling Esther's wagon'll travel a whole lot slower than I will, which makes your chances of being recognized better than mine even with my hat on your head. Now, let's stop talking and start moving."

As Wilcox slid down to the ground and climbed up on the wagon seat beside Esther, she slapped the rump of her horses with the reins and the wagon moved out.

So did Cimarron. At a gallop.

3

Cimarron was waiting well west of Fort Smith for Esther's wagon, and when it finally pulled up to him, he reached out and removed his hat from Ernie's head and clapped it on his own before moving out, the wagon traveling beside him.

"What will we do first when we reach McAlester?" Wilcox asked Cimarron. "The town's just up ahead of us."

"I see it," Cimarron said, not certain what answer he would give Wilcox. Then, "Esther, you told me back on the trail that the Widow Packer runs a dry-goods store. Where's it located?"

"In the business section of town. West of the Katy's tracks. Her name is on a sign outside it. Why do you ask, Cimarron? You're not going to cause trouble for Mr. Packer's mother, are you? Surely, you don't think she had anything to do with the gunning down of Mr. Labrette."

"Well, you mentioned to me a while ago that she thought the sun rose and set on her boy, Dan. Maybe she decided to do him a favor and move his competition for your hand out of his way."

"That's silly, Cimarron, and you know it," Esther declared heatedly. "Mrs. Packer is a sweet little old lady who wouldn't hurt a fly. And I told you when we first met that I was merely foolishly enamored of Dan Packer for a short time because he seemed so sophisticated—"

"Seemed to me to be a stuffed shirt," Wilcox interrupted, his tone sullen.

Esther ignored his outburst. "I told Dan Packer that I wanted nothing more to do with him. That I was in love with Ernie." She slipped her arm through Wilcox's and gave him a shy smile.

Cimarron said, "Now, what I want you two to do is go straight to your house, Esther, and stay there till I get there. If anybody sees you, Ernie, and asks any questions, why, you just act as slippery as ice on a millpond. Don't tell anybody what happened to you back in Fort Smith. Just let on that you're back in town and intending to stay here—with Esther."

"Stay with me?" Esther cried. "In my house? Unchaperoned? Cimarron, I can't do it. It would cause scandal for sure."

"You can do it," Cimarron insisted.

"I won't do it," Esther countered as they rode into town.

"You won't, won't you?" Cimarron gave her a sidelong glance as he rode on, his hands clasped around his saddle horn. "Well, if you won't, I have some serious doubts about whether my plan to help Ernie'll work out for the benefit of both of you."

Esther shifted position on the wagon seat. "I'll do it," she said so softly that the wind almost drowned out her words. "But my reputation will be ruined as a result."

"Maybe Ernie can save it. Maybe, if you play your cards right, he'll make an honest woman out of you."

"I *am* an honest woman!"

"Then stop wondering and worrying about what the folks in town'll have to say when they find out that you've got a man living with you without benefit of holy matrimony."

"They won't find out. I won't let Ernie out of the house. I'll draw all the shades and—"

"Oh, they'll find out, all right," Cimarron said. "On account of I intend to make it known about how you two've gone and set up housekeeping together."

"Cimarron, you wouldn't dare," Esther cried indignantly.

"I'm going to leave you two here now. I'll come by your

house a little later on, Esther." He sighed. "Ernie, I'm not usually an envying kind of man, but when I give thought to the two of you all alone together in that house with the shades all drawn down . . ." He sighed again, echoing the wind.

Esther turned away from him, blushing.

Wilcox laughed lightly and drove the wagon down the street.

Cimarron, when they had gone, turned his horse and crossed the tracks, heading for the town's business section.

Moments later, he drew rein in front of a modest store with an even more modest sign above its entrance that said: MRS. PACKER'S DRY GOODS.

He got out of the saddle and wrapped his reins around the hitch rail in front of the store. He stepped up on the boardwalk and entered the store, which he found was neither neat nor large. His eyes fell on the matronly woman—she's plump as a robin, he thought, and every bit as pert—who was bustling busily behind the counter to no apparent purpose that he could see.

"Oh!" she cried as, after suddenly bending down below her counter, she as suddenly rose and saw Cimarron standing, hands in the rear pockets of his jeans, staring at her. "A customer. What can I do for you, sir?"

"There's a lady I know who's hankering after a new dress. I figured maybe I'd pull a surprise on her. Buy her some yard goods to make one out of."

"Why, that's such a nice thought on your part, sir. What did you have in mind?"

"Beg pardon?" Cimarron strode over to the counter behind which the woman stood expectantly, his spurs clinking, his boots pounding the plank floor.

"What kind of goods did you have in mind? Something simple? Something fancy?"

"Well, I really couldn't say. The lady I'm thinking of" —an image of Jenny flashed in Cimarron's mind but was promptly banished by an image of her father and three brothers—"she dresses mostly modest."

45

"Calico?" The woman turned and took down a bolt of cloth from a shelf and then flopped it along the counter and fluffed up the freed material. "Does this seem suitable?"

"Well, ma'am—you're Mrs. Packer, I take it?"

"Yes, I am."

"You come—your store does—highly recommended to me." Cimarron took a handful of the calico and kneaded it between his lean fingers.

"Seventy cents a yard. Not expensive at all by most standards and really quite lovely. I could sell you some trim—not too showy, just right, lace?"

"Lace," Cimarron repeated.

"This material bastes quite easily. Is the lady in question a good seamstress?"

A mythical woman walked through the corridors of Cimarron's mind, and watching her, he said, "I reckon she is, and if she's not, she can learn to be." He paused and then, "Which is something Esther Lane's not likely to turn into. Not her with her uppity ways."

"You know Miss Lane?"

"Know her?" Cimarron muttered something—sounds, not words—and frowned. "She jilted me. Same as she's jilted other men, some better, some worse than me. I'll tell you something about Miss Esther Uppity Lane, Mrs. Packer. That woman turned me down in favor of a fuzz-faced boy who's barely been weaned. She did. That's a fact!"

"You must mean Ernie Wilcox."

"That's who I mean all right."

Mrs. Packer beamed at Cimarron. "They hanged Ernie Wilcox over in Fort Smith. I awaited the event with pleasure, I can tell you. My boy, Dan, did too because he intends to make Esther Lane his blushing bride now that Ernie Wilcox, that murderer, is dead and gone."

"I'm afraid you're wrong about Ernie, Mrs. Packer." Cimarron withdrew his hand from the calico. "I heard he didn't hang. In fact, I heard it said in town not more than a few minutes before I came in here that him and Esther Lane

46

are over at her house and that they intend to stay there, the pair of them, with or without the blessing of any preacher man.''

"No!" exclaimed Mrs. Packer. "You must be wrong. How could Ernie Wilcox be here and not hanged like he was supposed to be?"

Cimarron shrugged, raised his eyebrows, rolled his eyes.

Mrs. Packer hurried out from behind the counter, seized a paper sign, and hung it on the door. "I'm closing up now," she announced.

"But my woman—the dress she wanted so bad—"

"Some other time. Come back tomorrow." Mrs. Packer ripped off her apron and threw it on the counter. She waved both hands at Cimarron as if she were chasing chickens.

He turned and, grinning, left the store.

When Mrs. Packer came hurrying out of the store moments later, he was leaning, arms folded across his chest, against the wall next to the window. As she bent to turn the key in the door's lock, he crossed his booted ankles and said, "By the way, Mrs. Packer."

"Yes?" She looked up at him, pocketing her key.

"Your son—well, there's one other thing I heard in town that maybe he ought to know. Forgot to mention it to you before."

"Well, sir, what is it? I have things to do and you're holding me up."

"Folks say that Wilcox has more murdering on his mind. He appears to be a boastful man, from all I hear. Said the fact that he killed Labrette ought to stand as a warning to the rest of the men in McAlester and elsewhere who just might take it into their heads to come courting Esther Lane. Said he'd shoot the first and the last one and all those in between who tried that trick, and folks said he sounded like he meant every single word he said."

Mrs. Packer blanched. Her hands trembled. She skittered away across the street, her dark skirt billowing out behind her.

She's on her way to tend to the business she mentioned, Cimarron thought, opening his jackknife, which he had taken from his pocket, and idly picking his teeth with it. Her business that bears the name of her son, Dan Packer.

Cimarron snapped the jackknife shut, pocketed it, and strode down the boardwalk. When he reached the livery stable, he stood in the mouth of the alley that ran between the livery and the building next to it, stroking his chin and staring at the wild rose bushes at the far end of the alley. Everything looks the same, he thought, as when I last looked—the time I was here hunting for Ernie to bring him in on the charge of shooting and killing Labrette.

But now there was a difference. An unseen but definite difference about the alley and the rose bushes, as far as he was concerned. It could have happened that way, Cimarron mused. Maybe it did. And if it did happen that way, well, something else might be about to happen. To Ernie. To me too. Something dangerous.

He turned and was about to walk away when a sulky pulled up in front of the livery and the woman driving it stared at him, an expression of surprise on her face.

Cimarron touched the brim of his hat to her, noting her bright eyes, which were still on him, and her lush high-breasted and big-hipped body. She's got no more waist than a wasp, he thought. Wouldn't I like to put my hands around it and hold her still while I . . . She looks, were I to get her down on her back, as if I sure wouldn't have to use my spurs on her to prod her into action.

"You don't remember me," she said.

The woman's statement bordered on an accusation and it surprised Cimarron. "Should I remember you?"

"Well, that depends, I guess."

"On what?"

Her lips parted in a faint smile and then her smile grew bigger and brighter, revealing as it did so the gold in the center of her upper row of teeth.

The glint of gold in her smile did it. It dislodged a memory in Cimarron's mind and then he too was smiling and walking toward the sulky. "Goldy," he said softly when he reached it. "I reckon I deserve a sound thrashing for not remembering you right off. I must be getting old. Seems my mind's starting to play tricks on me."

"Well, I have changed the way I wear my hair and perhaps I've put on a pound or two."

"It was in Tishomingo down in Chickasaw Nation, wasn't it, the last time we met?"

"The last time we—met? Is that what you remember? Our meeting? Just that?"

"No, sirree, it's not, not by a long shot! I remember the way you can intoxicate a man so that in no time at all he don't know on which side of the world the sun rises and he sure don't give a hoot in hell on which side it sets."

"Oh, Cimarron, you look like a gunhawk, you walk like a mountain lion ready for the kill, but sometimes you talk as if you were born to turn the heads of every woman in the entire Territory."

"It's a faculty, I confess, that I cultivate. I've got to. What with this scar on my face and my knees and maybe more of me about to bust out of my jeans and being born with less brains than God gave gophers—well, a man like me has to find ways of getting around his many handicaps."

Goldy burst into laughter, causing her horse to prance and toss his head.

"What are you doing up here in Choctaw Nation, honey?" Cimarron asked her.

"Scandalizing all the churchgoing women in town and offering comfort to all the men. Same as usual. You know me, Cimarron. I'll never change."

"Is that a promise? I truly do hope it is because I happen to be a man in dire need of the kind of comfort you can offer."

"You never settled down, Cimarron? Never got married?"

Lila, Cimarron thought, and his body stiffened.

"What's wrong? Is something wrong, Cimarron?"

Cimarron, forcing himself to smile, said, "What in the

world could be wrong now that I've met up with you again so all of a sudden and unexpected like this and me with enough money in my jeans to pay whatever price you might happen to be asking for your comforting in these expensive modern times."

The ghost of his lost Lila Kane keened briefly in Cimarron's mind before vanishing.

"I'll see to your sulky, honey, and then—"

"And then it will be like old times for the two of us, Cimarron. Oh, I'm so very glad that I ran into you."

"You're a kindhearted woman, Goldy, to tell me such a bald-faced lie as that. Last time we were together, in case you've forgotten, you threw me out of that parlor house you were working in in Tishomingo after breaking a beer bottle on my head hard enough to crack my skull wide open."

"You were supposed to be with me, and when that hussy, Glenda, tried to take you away from me and you looked so damned willing to be taken— Well, you knew I had a temper, Cimarron, so what happened is your own fault."

"Reckon you're right. Here, I'll help you step down."

"You're as gallant as ever." Goldy took Cimarron's hand and stepped down from the sulky.

He released her, went up to her horse, and gripping its bridle, led the animal into the dim interior of the livery.

When he returned to Goldy, she took his arm and said, "I have a room in the hotel in town."

They made their way to it, talking of the good times they had shared together in the past, and once inside Goldy's room, Cimarron slammed the door shut behind him and seized her.

When their kiss ended, Goldy, breathless, whispered, "Some things never change. You don't, Cimarron. You're as much of a man now—maybe more of one—than you were that last time we were together in Tishomingo."

Cimarron threw his hat and then his bandanna on a chair and began to unbutton his shirt. "You've got only yourself to blame for that, Goldy. Why, only a sissy wouldn't go stiff at the very first sight of a wonderful woman like yourself."

Cimarron, as he unstrapped his cartridge belt and draped it over the back of the chair beside the bed, watched Goldy slip out of her blouse and then let her skirt drift down to the floor. His eyes were still on her as she stepped out of the frothy puddle of her skirt and turned her back to him.

"Unlace my stays," she whispered, and he moved up to her and did so, his fingers fumbling as desire for her shuddered through him.

She tossed her corset aside, kicked off her shoes, and bent over to roll down her stockings.

Cimarron, his eyes roving from her breasts to the dark thatch between her legs, sat down on the bed and pulled off his boots. He was up on his feet then and getting out of his pants, and he was more than ready for Goldy when she reached out to him and he, stone-stiff, entered her arms and felt them enclose him in their warm embrace.

He throbbed against her bare body as they kissed, and a moment after she took his tongue and began to suck on it, he felt drops of fluid ooze from his erection to moisten her seductively undulating belly.

"Cimarron, you didn't—"

As Goldy drew away from him, ending their kiss, he shook his head. "Not yet. That wetness you feel, it just shows how ready I am. Not to mention how eager." He led her to the bed, and after she lay down upon it, he put one knee on it and a moment later he was straddling her, kneeling on the bed and gazing down with deep longing at the ripe and faintly trembling body beneath him.

Goldy reached up and ran an index finger along the underside of his shaft. "It's even bigger than I remember."

"You're even more beautiful than I remembered you being, honey." He bent over and kissed her breasts, one after the other, and then began to suck the one on his left. As Goldy's nipple hardened, he teased it with his tongue a moment and then did the same to her left breast. He felt her hand tighten around him and begin to stroke him gently.

Then her other hand rose and cupped his testicles, causing his scrotum to shrink as pleasure coursed like a river filled with rapids throughout his body.

He straightened and then lowered himself upon her, probing gently, his hands on her shoulders, his lips nuzzling her earlobes.

He thrust a small part of himself into her. He withdrew. And then thrust more of himself into her. Withdrew again.

Goldy moaned, her head tossing from one side of the pillow beneath it to the other.

"You're a tease," she murmured. "Such a wonderful tease!"

"Just want to make sure I'm not the only one who gets pleasured, honey. Just want to make sure you do too."

Her pelvis rose to meet his and Cimarron found himself almost all the way inside the slippery wetness of her. The time for teasing, he knew, was over. The time for the two of them to know the exhilarating triumph of their being together like this was at hand.

He plunged into her, forcing her pelvis back down on the bed and causing a sigh to escape from her lips as her arms encircled him.

Her legs scissored themselves around his thighs as she began to sweat, whispering, "You're so good . . . so damned good!"

Her sudden cry fled past his ear as her body shook beneath his. Her fingernails dug into his back.

The room and the world of which it was a part vanished for Cimarron and there was left only their joined loins, which existed in a hot void as he rose, fell, rose again, and then plunged down one final time and erupted within her.

He continued his by-now-uncontrollable plunging, his chest heaving, his breath coming in short sharp gasps as he flooded her.

Finally, with one last body-bending spasm, he lay still upon her, conscious of her breasts pressing against his sweat-slick chest, of her breath sliding sibilantly past his ears, of his still-stiff erection impaling her where she lay with her arms and legs still wrapped tightly around him.

He raised his head and kissed the base of her throat.

"It was wonderful," Goldy whispered. "It feels so good to be so relaxed. So peaceful. As if everything's right with the world."

Her words triggered the reality in Cimarron's mind that had been held at bay during their lovemaking. He slowly withdrew from her and sat down on the edge of the bed.

A moment later, as he stood up and started to dress, Goldy turned toward him and said, "You're not leaving, I hope."

"Got to, honey."

"When will you come back?"

"Can't say when exactly."

Goldy's lower lip thrust outward in a pout. "You are without a doubt harder to hold in a single place than the sun itself." She propped her head up with one hand and said, "Once more, Cimarron."

"Not now, honey. I've got a matter that needs seeing to real bad." He pulled on his jeans and then his boots.

"I need seeing to—by you. At least once more. You can do it once more, can't you? You always used to be able to do it over and over again without so much as taking time to breathe in between."

"I still am able to, I reckon. But like I said, I've got something mighty important to tend to. But now that I know where you are, I'll look you up first chance I get." He put on his shirt, buttoned it, then tied his bandanna around his neck and tossed a folded ten-dollar bill on the bed.

"You won't oblige me, then?"

"Not right now, though I'd truly like to. Some other time when I've got the time to be obliging, which right now I don't have."

"*Now!*" Goldy demanded angrily. "Right this very minute!"

Cimarron, after he had strapped his cartridge belt around his hips and clapped his hat on his head, bent down and kissed her. "Next time I'm lucky enough to get together with you, we'll do it a bit different. You remember how?" He ran an index finger along the line of her lips. "You were always at your best when it came to taking me in your mouth."

Goldy slapped his face.

Cimarron stepped back from the bed. "Honey, you've got to try to understand. The business I've got to be about, it's likely to turn out to be a matter of life and death."

Goldy, without a word, picked up a cut-glass compote dish that sat on the table beside the bed and threw it at him.

He ducked in time and it missed him. Grinning, he warned, "Now, you'd better hold a tight rein on that temper of yours, honey, or I'm liable to get hurt where I'll wind up without the means to repeat my last little performance with you."

Goldy picked up an unlighted coal oil lamp and threw it at him.

It struck him on the shoulder, and as it crashed on the floor, he bounded across the room to the door. He opened it, turned, blew Goldy a kiss, and then slammed it.

He ran down the hall, down the stairs, and out into the street.

He sprinted the entire distance to Mrs. Packer's dry-goods store, where he freed his horse and swung into the saddle. Riding hard down the street, he soon found himself in front of Esther's house. He dismounted and went up to her door and knocked on it.

When she opened it, he stepped past her and closed the door behind him. "Ernie's here?"

"In the kitchen," she said, and led him to where Wilcox was seated at the kitchen table eating a huge piece of mince-meat pie.

"Will you have some?" Esther asked Cimarron, reaching for the pie. "Some coffee?"

"Both'd be fine." He sat down at the table and said, "Ernie, I had me a talk with the Widow Packer. Now, I've gone and put you on the spot, so what I want you and Esther to do is get out of here right now. Go hole up somewhere safe till I tell you it's all right for you to come back."

"What do you mean about putting me on the spot?" Ernie asked.

"I told Mrs. Packer that you were here with Esther," Cimarron answered as she placed pie and coffee in front of him and then sat down beside him at the table. "I told her that you'd put out the word that anybody who came calling on Esther would get a bullet from you by way of a warning to stay away from the woman you'd staked your claim on."

"What did you do that for?" Esther cried anxiously. "Ernie's in enough trouble as it is without you spreading lies about him, Cimarron."

"I did it, Esther, because I had a good reason to do it. Ernie, answer me a question. That gun I took away from you the night I caught up with you—that Wilcox 1849 Model thirty-one-caliber revolver—was that the one you used in your gun duel with Labrette?"

"Yes. Why?"

"You were standing up when you fired at him?"

"Sure, I was. I was down at the end of the alley when he challenged me—"

"With those wild rose bushes behind you? You were standing up—not even crouching a little bit?"

"No, I wasn't crouching."

"You know that Labrette was gut-shot, don't you?"

Ernie nodded.

"I don't see what you're getting at, Cimarron," Esther remarked.

"What I'm getting at is this. I had me a look down that alley—twice. The first time was when I came here hunting Ernie. The second time was a little while ago. Now, Ernie says he was standing up, not even crouching, when he fired at Labrette."

"Labrette fired first," Ernie interjected.

"When I was here the first time," Cimarron continued, "the owner of the livery told me that Labrette was a short man. He said he was gut-shot, but it seemed to him that Labrette should have gotten it in the lungs because, as he put it to me, 'Labrette, he was such a little fella. Dapper but small of stature.' When I found out from Esther back in Fort Smith that Labrette had been killed by a forty-five, I figured the shooting mustn't've happened the way folks thought it did. Since then, I've been thinking that somebody else must have shot Labrette, because your ammunition was thirty-one caliber and because, if you had shot a man of small stature, you most likely would have hit him in the lungs like the man from the livery said or maybe even in the head.''

"But there was nobody else in the alley but us," Ernie declared.

"Maybe you're right about that and maybe you're wrong. Maybe there was somebody else.''

"I would have seen him.''

"Did you look behind you?''

"Behind me?''

"At the rose bushes?''

"No.''

"Then maybe somebody could have been hiding behind them. They're low-growing. That somebody's forty-five would have hit Labrette in the gut if that somebody was down flat on the ground so as not to be seen by anybody.''

"But who could it have been?'' Esther asked.

"Dan Packer," Ernie breathed.

"You got it," Cimarron said, and forked pie into his mouth, which he washed down with a swallow of coffee.

"He was in love with Esther too," Ernie said.

"So that's why you told Mrs. Packer those lies about Ernie," Esther said, her eyes widening as she stared at Cimarron. "It was to goad Dan Packer into—''

"Making a move," Cimarron interrupted. "If he's the one who shot Labrette—and I happen to think he is the one—he's likely to try again to take you down, Ernie. That's why I want you two out of here for the time being. I don't want either one of you hurt should Packer come gunning for his rival in his affair of the heart.''

"The black-hearted bastard!" Wilcox exclaimed.

"Ernie!" Esther cried. "Such language!"

"Is there a place the two of you can go to until we see if Packer takes the bait I gave his ma to put out for him?"

"I have a friend who lives on the other side of town," Esther said. "Her name is Dolores Johnson. She lives with her parents. We could go there."

"Go now," Cimarron ordered, finishing his pie and coffee. "Wait there until you hear from me."

"You're staying here?" Wilcox asked.

"I am if that's all right with you, Esther."

"It's all right," Esther said.

"I'm staying here too," Wilcox announced.

Cimarron tried arguing with him, but Wilcox doggedly insisted on staying, claiming that he had a right to face up to any trouble that might be coming because, as he put it, "It's my neck that's at stake in this matter."

Cimarron gave up on his efforts to persuade Wilcox to leave. Later, after Esther had gone and dusk began to settle on McAlester, he went into the kitchen to make fresh coffee, leaving Wilcox sitting alone and tense in the front parlor of the house.

The coffee had just begun to boil when he heard the front door open and a man's voice mutter, "Don't move, Wilcox. I'll shoot you if you do."

Cimarron flattened his back against the wall next to the door leading to the kitchen and listened as Wilcox said, "Packer, you bastard—"

"Shut up!" Packer barked. "Now, you and I are going to walk outside—out the back door and into the dark where I'm going to shoot you because you tried to escape from me after I captured you.

"I'll be a local hero, Wilcox, as a result of my bravery and just think how my new status will impress Esther. When my mother told me you were in town, I made up my mind to kill you and I'm going to kill you."

"Like you killed Labrette," Wilcox said.

"On your feet, Wilcox, and head for the back door."

Cimarron eased the kitchen door around so that it hid him from the sight of anyone entering the kitchen. He unleathered his .44 and eased its hammer back.

"Sure, I killed Labrette," Packer was saying as the sound of his and Wilcox's footsteps sounded in the parlor. "I was right there that day—hiding behind the rose bushes at the end of the alley. I saw your gunfight as a way for me to get rid of two birds with one stone, so to speak. I made it look as if you had killed Labrette and I figured the law would kill you for that rash act. What happened, Wilcox? How did you get out of jail?"

Cimarron tensed as two sets of footsteps sounded in the kitchen. At the sound of the outside kitchen door opening, he stepped out from behind the door leading to the kitchen and said, "Drop your gun, Packer."

Packer froze.

Wilcox spun around and ripped Packer's revolver from the man's hand.

A woman screamed from somewhere behind Cimarron.

"Mister, put that gun away," a male voice said from behind Cimarron. "There's going to be no gunplay here tonight."

Cimarron placed his gun on the kitchen table and slowly turned around to find himself facing a man wearing a tin star behind whom stood a pale Mrs. Packer.

"Sheriff," Packer said, "I caught him." He gestured at Wilcox and reached for his gun, which was in Wilcox's hand, but Wilcox stepped around him and placed the gun on the kitchen table beside Cimarron's. "You recognize Wilcox, don't you, Sheriff?" Packer continued, smiling uncertainly. "Somehow or other he managed to escape from the jail in Fort Smith."

"I know he did," the sheriff said flatly. "When Mrs. Packer came to me and told me that you were coming here to try to capture Wilcox on your own, I came after him at her urging so that you wouldn't get hurt."

"He's going to get hurt, though, Packer is," Cimarron commented. "He killed Labrette, Sheriff. Ernie didn't."

"I heard him confess to the murder just now," the sheriff said. "Let's go, Packer."

"No!" Mrs. Packer cried. She ran across the kitchen and threw her arms around Packer. "My boy never killed anyone!"

"Why did you have to go to the sheriff, Mother?" Packer snapped, pushing her away from him so that she stood in the middle of the kitchen, her alarmed eyes on her angry son.

"I wanted to protect you," she whimpered, wringing her hands.

"Protect me!" Packer screamed. "All you've ever done for me was meddle in my life so that at times I swear I felt like you were smothering me! Now you've—you've *killed* me!"

"Run!" Mrs. Packer cried, seizing her son's gun from the table and aiming it at the sheriff. She pulled the trigger and a shot slammed into the wall not far from where the sheriff stood.

Wilcox sprang forward and wrested the gun from her hand before she could fire again, and Cimarron sprinted through the outside kitchen door after Packer, who had fled.

He leaped on the man and brought him down to the ground. Then he got up and dragged Packer back into the kitchen. "He's all yours, Sheriff."

"Who are you?" the sheriff asked.

Cimarron shoved a hand into a pocket of his jeans and came up with his nickel star. "We're two of a kind, Sheriff, you and me. You're a sheriff and I'm a deputy marshal from Judge Parker's court in Fort Smith."

"Oh, Dan!" wailed Mrs. Packer as the sheriff, grim-faced, accepted Packer's gun from Wilcox and thrust it into his belt.

"Looks like you told the truth at your trial," the sheriff said, and Wilcox nodded. "I'll tell you something. You never did strike me as the killing kind."

"He's not," Cimarron told the sheriff. "Now you'd best

59

telegraph to Fort Smith. Tell them to send a deputy here to take Packer back for trial on a charge of murdering Labrette and trying to murder Wilcox. You can keep him cooped up in your jail till the deputy gets here. Tell Marshal Upham in Fort Smith to send along summonses for Wilcox, Mrs. Packer, and yourself to testify at Packer's trial.''

Mrs. Packer fainted, falling in a fat heap on the floor at her son's feet.

"Tell Upham I'll testify too at the trial," Cimarron added.

"Why don't you save me all that trouble, Deputy, and take Packer back to Fort Smith yourself?''

"On account of I'm assigned to escort a circus to the Texas border, so I can't. Which reminds me. Who do I see about getting a license so that the circus can put on a show here in McAlester?''

"Me.''

"I'll be in your office first thing in the morning to get that license, Sheriff.''

Mrs. Packer regained consciousness, struggled to her feet, and fled after the sheriff, who was marching her son out of the house and into the night.

"I don't know how to thank you for all you've done for me, Cimarron," Wilcox said.

"I'm in no need of thanks for what I did," Cimarron remarked, picking up his revolver from the table and holstering it.

"When I think what could have happened to me—damn nearly did, but didn't because of you—I get cold chills.''

"Esther might be able to chase away those cold chills of yours.''

"I've got to tell her what happened," Wilcox exclaimed happily. "Come with me, Cimarron. We'll both tell her.''

Cimarron shook his head. "I've got other plans. You go ahead and tell her. And tell her I'm real glad things worked out the way they did.''

After Wilcox had run from the room, Cimarron left the

house and headed back to the hotel and Goldy, hoping there was nothing else left in her room that she could throw at him before they got down to the important business of making her bed bounce once again.

4

The following night, as Cimarron left the circus wagon he had been given for his private quarters and stepped out onto the backyard, he made his way around the big top and was heading for its entrance when he heard the loud argument taking place between Simpson and the young man who was standing behind the half-door of the ticket wagon.

As the half-door swung open and the man in the wagon jumped down to the ground and took a swing at Simpson, Cimarron ran over to the pair and seized Simpson's attacker from behind.

"Let go!" the man yelled, and broke free of Cimarron.

"I warned you," Simpson yelled at the man. "Twice I warned you. But you persisted in your shenanigans and I'll have no more of them. You're through, Crocker! Get off the lot, and get off it fast. I don't want to see you here when tonight's show is over—or ever again for that matter."

"I told you, Simpson, that we could split the take between us."

"No," Simpson thundered. "I run a clean show. A decent show. I won't have the people who come to see it cheated the way you were cheating them, Crocker."

"Who cheated them? I didn't cheat them. All I did—"

"I know what you did and I won't have you doing it ever again. Now get out of here."

Crocker swung and his left fist cracked against Simpson's jaw, sending the elderly man stumbling backward.

Cimarron seized Crocker, spun him around, and landed a hard pair of body blows that emptied Crocker's lungs of air and caused him to double over in a fit of wheezy coughing.

"You heard the gaffer, Crocker," Cimarron said. "You're fired. You want to argue the point, argue it with me and not with a man twice your age who can't fight back the way I can."

Crocker, still coughing and still bent over, managed to curse both Cimarron and Simpson resoundingly. "I'll fix you, Simpson," he finally bellowed when his coughing subsided. "You just wait. You'll see. I'll even things up between us."

Then, as Crocker shambled away and out of sight, Cimarron crossed over to where Simpson stood. "You all right?"

Simpson nodded. "That Crocker could have caused us even more trouble with the law."

"What was he doing that you didn't like?"

"Opening the wagon early and charging the suckers extra for a reserved seat. Some of them want to be sure of getting in and are willing to pay a premium to men like Crocker. He was keeping the extra money for himself. I caught on to what he was doing even before we reached Fort Smith and I warned him that if he kept it up he was finished. Well, now he is finished. I thank you, Cimarron, for your help. And for getting us our reader."

"Beg pardon?"

Simpson smiled. "A reader's a license to work a town."

"It was no trouble. None at all." Cimarron paused a moment and then, "What did you mean before when you said that Crocker could have caused more trouble with the law. You've already had some?"

"We did. Johnny Tin Plate was here this afternoon making some noise and generally making a nuisance of himself. It became clear to me early on that he had his nose out of joint because the bank in McAlester, according to him, had been robbed this afternoon and he hadn't the slightest notion of who did the deed. So he tried to vent his spleen against us. What I should have done then was turn Crocker over to him for being a cake cutter.''

"Cake cutter?''

"Shortchange artist. But I didn't. Instead, I gave him five passes for tonight's show and he went away somewhat mollified.''

From the big top came the music of the brass band, which blended with enthusiastic applause.

"Why don't you go on in and see the show, Cimarron?''

"I was on my way to do just that.''

"Enjoy it,'' Simpson called out as Cimarron made his way to the tent's entrance.

"Ticket, please.''

Cimarron pulled his badge from his pocket and showed it to the ticket taker. "Maybe you've heard about me. I'm the Johnny Tin Plate that's going to guide you folks across Indian Territory. Figured that might get me in to see the show for free.''

"Sure it will,'' the ticket taker said. "I have heard about you and I'm glad to have you with us, Marshal. I've not got the slightest hankering to get myself scalped by any redskin out here in this hellhole.''

Cimarron entered the big top and took up a position in a wide aisle between two sloping tiers of seats and began to watch the gaudy pageant that was Simpson's Colossal Circus swirl past his dazzled eyes.

Two men in chariots, each pulled by teams of two horses, raced furiously down the hippodrome track, their Roman togas flying out behind their heels. They swiftly turned and raced back again and then out of the tent to the applause of the townspeople filling the seats. In the single ring two clowns, wearing fright wigs and baggy pants supported by bright-orange galluses, pretended to fight, their hands covered by gigantic boxing gloves. As one of them was knocked down by the other, the people in the audience roared with laughter and then roared even louder as the downed clown bounced back to his feet, swung a huge glove, and knocked the papier-mâché head off the other clown, who ran, apparently decapitated, from the ring and out of the tent.

Cimarron turned and studied the faces of the spectators, all of them alive with mirth, their eyes wide as if they wanted to make absolutely certain they missed nothing, *oohhhs* and *aahhhs* issuing from their lips as Ramona Bertolini, resplendent in a short pink costume that hugged her lithe body, walked the taut rope high above their heads, an equally pink parasol held high in her right hand, a confident smile on her pretty face as her satin-slippered feet slid along the rope beneath them.

Cimarron watched a child no more than five years old stuff two pieces of candy into her mouth and then spit both of them out as she cried out in surprised delight at the sight of the show's two elephants, howdahs on their backs and veiled women waving from the howdahs. The elephants lumbered down the hippodrome track followed by capering clowns, who were in turn followed by four somersaulting tumblers in white tights.

The band switched to a livelier tune and high above the audience Ramona's parasol wavered, but she did not. When she had completed her journey across the rope to the tiny platform that had been her destination, she bowed gracefully to the people applauding below her and the band played a musical flourish to salute her.

The people in the audience stared up at her like so many subjects adoring their indomitable queen, who had just made their lives a little brighter and their hearts a little lighter as a result of her willingness to risk death or possible injury in an effort to entertain them. They watched Ramona bow and blow kisses to them with glowing eyes that were grateful for the hidden truth that she had given them, the truth that promised them that lives need not to be lived dully. Their faces shone in the light drifting down from the candles and coal-oil lamps fastened to the tent poles as they gazed raptly up at Ramona, who had just given them all the sudden and energizing hope that their lives too might be filled with color and delight someday, were they to become like Ramona herself, willing to dare the world every day and win.

Seduced by the music, the color, the gaiety, and the gaudy beauty of the circus, Cimarron forgot the world beyond the canvas walls and found himself staring through the eyes of the boy he had once been and seeing—magic. Listening with that long-lost boy's ears, he heard not merely a brass band but glorious music that summoned more and more marvels— dogs dancing on their hind legs; a bear dressed as a ballet dancer; women with brightly painted eyes and mouths and cheeks; men both strong and secure in their youth and adroit agility who stood like towers, one upon the other's shoulders, until they almost touched the canvas sky above them; a clown pushing a baby in a carriage who wore a frilly blue dress and bluer cap and who then, not wanting any longer to be a baby, jumped out of the carriage and went running away on all four of its pig's feet with the clown chasing frantically after it and falling forlorn into a tub of water.

Cimarron laughed uproariously as a drunk in the audience, his pants threatening to fall down at any moment, claimed loudly and abusively that he could ride the dapple cantering beneath a male equestrian in the ring better "than any fancy-pants mister who wouldn't know good riding from rope-skipping."

Cimarron watched as the drunk climbed down from his seat in the audience and staggered into the ring. He was as amazed as everyone else when the drunk leaped up behind the horse's rider and the original rider jumped to the ground and the drunk kicked off his falling pants, tore off his shirt, tossed it aside, and then, dressed in spangled tights, did a handstand on the cantering dapple's broad back.

He cheered the man along with the rest of the crowd, delighted to have been deceived, swiftly becoming aware that the circus was a world where not everything was what it seemed to be, a world where wonders were the order of the day, one where ordinary reality wore a pale face compared to the bright one beneath the big top, one where babies could turn into pigs and drunks into bareback riders in the wink of a startled eye.

He watched the first of the snarling lions and leopards glide through the slat-sided wooden chute next to him and into the iron-barred arena that had been constructed in the ring by the roustabouts following the departure of the dapple and the two equestrians who had been riding it.

His eyes turned to Gunther von Kleist, who stood in the center of the arena, bare-chested and black-booted, a long leather whip in his right hand.

Gunther moved into the center of the arena, his supple muscles rippling, his eyes on his cats. He raised the whip and snapped it. A lion leaped up onto a low platform. Gunther gave a guttural command and a flick of his whip and two leopards leaped up to take positions a little below and on both sides of the lion.

Six ears fell back to lie flat against three snarling skulls. Three mouths opened to reveal gleaming white fangs. One leopard raised a paw and viciously clawed the air, its yellow eyes on Gunther, who was moving about the arena, swiftly positioning his cats, forcing them to ride brightly painted barrels they rolled beneath their paws, forcing them to rear up on their hind legs and roar, forcing them finally to leap, one after the other, through a blazing hoop of fire he held aloft as he shouted his commands in German to his obedient beasts.

The crowd and Cimarron went wild at this demonstration of the superiority of one man over a cageful of abjectly submissive wild animals that were, as the closing element of Gunther's act illustrated, completely subservient to the blond giant who stood so godlike before them.

Later, after Gunther had guided the last of his cats back into the chute on their way to their cages and the iron bars had been dismantled, the band began to play a lilting melody, one Cimarron had never heard before.

The ring was empty now, as was the hippodrome track.

The audience, their eyes fixed on the flap covering the entrance to the big top, waited expectantly.

Then, when the waiting had begun to seem interminable to Cimarron, the flap was drawn back and Lucinda, astride the most beautiful white horse he had ever seen, moved at a stately pace down the hippodrome track toward the center ring.

She was wearing a full-skirted ankle-length dress that flowed down both sides of her mount. Her stunningly simple dress was as white as her Lipizzaner. Her reins rested lightly in her kid-gloved hands. Her eyes were bright beneath the glittering jeweled tiara she wore on her head, almost as bright as those of the great dark eyes of the stallion she was riding.

"Oh, my," Cimarron heard a woman seated near him sigh. "Look, Jim. Isn't she lovely?"

Cimarron turned and saw the man named Jim nod mutely, his eyes riveted on Lucinda.

She's more than lovely, he thought as he turned his attention back to her and she rode the length of the hippodrome track and then into the ring. She's something a man might've dreamed up. She looks like something out of a storybook. Even in that dress that hides her body from her shoulders to her shoes, she's a woman a man would want any way he could have her. She's woman enough to rouse lust in a eunuch.

"That's the *piaffe*," said a gruff voice beside Cimarron as the Lipizzaner beneath Lucinda performed a cadenced trot in place, its haunches deeply bent.

He turned to find Gunther, a long satin cape draped over his broad shoulders, standing beside him. "*Piaffe*," Cimarron repeated. "That's French, I take it."

"Yes. See that—*pesade*."

"How the hell does she get that horse to do all that? She doesn't move a muscle, far as I can see."

"Little touches of her legs. Her knees. On the reins she tugs at times but it is hard to see. That is the point of *haute école.* For the rider to guide the horse without seeming to do so.''

Cimarron watched, frankly admiring, as Lucinda's stallion cantered in a long glide that was the most graceful movement he had ever seen a horse make, and then proceeded to trot sideward.

He continued watching her, seeing her not only as a wholly desirable woman now but also as an expert rider.

''That is the end of the on-the-ground part,'' said Gunther. ''Now, the above-ground steps.''

Lucinda, her face impassive, remained almost immobile as her Lipizzaner leaped into the air, all four of its feet off the ground, its front legs curled close to its chest, its hind legs kicking out behind its body.

''That sure is some beautiful sight,'' Cimarron commented.

''It is called a *capriole,* that step,'' declared Gunther.

The audience applauded and continued applauding as the stallion, with no apparent direction from Lucinda, rose up on its hind legs, its front legs up in the air, and began to jump forward in a series of short hops.

''That there's got a name too, has it?'' Cimarron asked Gunther.

''It is called a *courbette.*''

After Lucinda, smiling now, had moved the Lipizzaner out of the ring, both horse and rider bowed to the audience. And then, her long white dress rippling against the ribs of the Lipizzaner, she trotted in stately fashion down the hippodrome track and out from under the big top.

''She is good, yes?'' prodded Gunther.

''Better than good by a country mile. She—her and that horse—they make a tip-top team.''

''I think so too.''

''You like that stallion of hers, do you?'' Cimarron inquired, a mischievous glint in his eye.

''It is a good horse.''

''And Lucinda?''

"A good woman. A beautiful woman. As you say in English, she is—magnif—magnifical?"

"Magnificent."

"Yes, that is it. Lucinda is magnificent."

Cimarron had to agree with Gunther. "You put on quite a show yourself with those big cats of yours. Any one of them looked like he could eat a man twice your size and then ask for seconds."

A lone cowboy in pursuit of three Indians thundered down the hippodrome track, firing his two guns in the air and whooping at the top of his voice.

"It is in knowing how to make the cats obey," Gunther said. "A man can learn how."

"Not this man," Cimarron said. "I wouldn't fancy studying how to tame those beasts of yours."

Gunther frowned as the Indians attacked a Conestoga wagon at the far end of the track that was being driven by Matt Ledman, who was now wearing trail driver's clothes. As the cowboy continued firing and a woman inside the wagon screamed at the top of her voice, the audience cheered the cowboy on.

"I would not like to learn to be a deputy marshal," Gunther said. "I would not like to have men shoot at me."

"It's each man to his own taste, I guess."

"Yes," Gunther said, and a moment later he was gone.

When the woman in the wagon had been rescued from the Indians by the cowboy, the band burst into a rousing rendition of "The Star-Spangled Banner" and the audience began to file out of the big top, carrying sleepy children and talking happily among themselves.

Cimarron left the tent and went around to the backyard, where he immediately spotted Lucinda, who was dressed now in a blouse and skirt.

Facing her was Gunther, and the two of them seemed to be arguing, Cimarron noticed. He halted, although he had wanted to find her so that he could tell her how much he had admired her performance. He saw Gunther grip her arms and lean down toward her. He saw Lucinda move momentarily closer to Gunther and then away from him. He watched as she shook herself free and he saw Gunther reach for her again.

She eluded him and was about to walk away when she suddenly stopped and then almost indolently reached up and placed her arms around Gunther's neck and pressed her lips against his.

Gunther's arms went around her, and as he drew her close to him, his satin cape almost completely enveloped her.

"That man is a fool," Ramona Bertolini snapped as she appeared at Cimarron's side.

"He looks like a mighty lucky man to me, fool though he may be in your opinion."

"Lucky," Ramona exclaimed. "To try to make love to that tease—that tart?"

Cimarron glanced at Ramona, noting her angry eyes as she stood with her hands on her hips staring at the pair locked together in the distance.

She turned and walked away from him, tossing her hair, her fists balled at her sides.

Lucinda pushed Gunther away and then walked away from him, leaving him standing behind her with a perplexed expression on his face.

So that's how the land lies, Cimarron thought. She's not all that interested in Gunther. She must have seen Ramona coming up behind me and decided to give in to Gunther to make Ramona mad.

Cimarron ran around behind one of the wagons and managed to intercept Lucinda, who halted when she saw him and smiled sweetly.

"Did you like the show?" she inquired sweetly.

"How'd you know I saw it?"

"I noticed you standing in the aisle. You're a man who tends to stand out in a crowd."

"Thought you did a real fine job with that horse of yours. Couldn't hardly make up my mind which one of the pair of you was the most beautiful."

71

"Did you finally reach a decision?"

"I just lied to you."

"You did?" Lucinda reached up and unbuttoned the top two buttons of Cimarron's shirt, letting her cool hand rest against his bared chest.

"The truth of the matter is I decided that you were the most beautiful a whole lot quicker'n a stuttering man can shout 'shucks,' though that horse of yours is a beauty too."

"He is a fine animal," Lucinda agreed, a faint smile lifting the corners of her mouth. Her hand gently slid along Cimarron's chest. "He and I get along quite well together. I suppose you could say that I'm fortunate insofar as I seem to have a way with stallions."

"Seems to me the stallions you have your way with are the fortunate ones."

"I do try hard to treat them right."

"Lucinda, honey, if you were to treat them wrong, I reckon they'd still be happier with you than with any other woman who treated them right."

"The show's coming down," Lucinda observed, withdrawing her hand.

Cimarron became aware of the elephants straining at the ends of chains and the clatter of candy and food stands being broken down and loaded on wagons. Behind him roustabouts worked to bring the big top down.

He turned to watch them straining on the ropes and poles, and when he turned back, Lucinda had vanished.

As a roustabout passed him, he hailed the man and asked, "Where and how might it be best for me to lend a hand in getting the show on the trail?"

"See him," the roustabout responded, pointing to a thickly bearded man standing near a group of men who were folding the big top that had just been lowered to the ground with a loud *whoossh*. "He's the boss hostler. Talk to him."

Cimarron strode over to the man and said, "I'm—"

"I know who you are," the man interrupted. "I don't know what you want with me."

"There's no good reason, I don't think, for you to be suspicious of me, mister, just because I happen to be a lawman. I'd like to lend you a hand."

"I'm Scott," the hostler said. "You want work, you got it. You can help load the canvas, supplies, and heavy equipment on the baggage train. It'll move out first. The cage train will follow and then the rest of the wagons."

"You know where you're headed, I take it."

"I know," Scott said. "The gaffer told me what you told him earlier today. We move west."

"That's all Simpson told you?"

"He said to keep the Canadian River on our right and the Military Road on our left."

"You got it. Now, maybe I should mention that you'll be traveling across open prairie for a spell, and that's easy. But then you'll come to the Sandstone Hills, and that's not so easy because those hills, they run roughly in a north-south direction and we'll have to haul ourselves up and over them, one after the other."

"My teamsters are good men. They'll manage. We'll send a man up ahead with a lantern, and if he spots any tricky terrain, he'll stick a torch in the ground and light it to show us the way."

Cimarron nodded and then joined the roustabouts in their task of folding up the big top. Later, he helped lash it and store its sections in wagons. Still later—he looked up at the stars and from their position knew that it was after midnight—he helped load light carriages, carts, and carryalls that moved out behind the bandwagon and the wagons carrying caged animals and the elephants with their keepers walking beside them, bull hooks in their hands.

He went to the wagon he had been given, made sure his black was safely tied to its rear end, and then climbed up on its seat and moved his team out.

When the lights of McAlester had vanished behind the cavalcade, he drove his team behind the cage train. In the sky above him, clouds began to obscure the moon and many of the stars, causing the darkness shrouding the prairie to deepen. Ahead of him, he spotted a torch burning dimly, and when he and the bandwagon reached the spot where it blazed, he saw that it marked a steeply rising hill of badly eroded shale and sandstone. As the bandwagon detoured around the hill, so did Cimarron. He drove on, conscious of the thudding of the elephants just behind him, of the bandwagon driver dozing as he drove and then snapping awake only to doze again, of the creaking wheels of the cage train and the occasional roar of one of Gunther's cats that invaded the night, which was now almost starless because of the thickening clouds in the sky overhead.

As he drove on, the minutes aged into hours. He searched the sky for traces of false dawn's first light, but it did not appear. He gradually became aware of a new sound in the night, one he had not heard before, a dull rhythmic sound that resembled a grumble.

He realized that it was coming from inside his wagon at the same instant that he recognized it for what it was—the sonorous sound of someone snoring.

Somebody's in my wagon, he thought. Didn't know—wasn't told I'd have to share it. Matter of fact, the gaffer, when he told me I could use it, mentioned something about it being mine alone. Then who . . . ?

Lucinda, he hoped. She's sneaked into my wagon to surprise me, figuring somebody'd spell me on the driving at some point tonight and then her and me, we could . . .

I sure am one for wishing the world into a shape that suits me, he thought with a grin. But that doesn't change the fact that somebody's in there and doesn't belong there.

"Whoa!" he said to his team, and when they halted, he braked the wagon, stepped down on the wheel hub and then down to the ground. He went around to the back of the wagon and opened its rear door to confront the blackness that dwelled within it.

The snoring was louder now and he climbed up and into the wagon, feeling about for a lamp. He found a body.

It groaned and turned over.

He shook it roughly.

It groaned again and he shook it even more roughly.

"Hey!" a male voice cried. "What—"

"Who the hell are you? This here's my wagon. What're you doing in my bunk?"

"Sleeping. What's it look to you like I'm doing?"

Cimarron picked up the man and threw him through the door and then he climbed out of the wagon to stare down at the man, who was moaning on the ground by his boots.

That's no man, he thought. He's but a boy.

"You didn't have to treat me so rough," the boy on the ground whimpered. "I would have gotten out on my own if you'd let me."

"Who the hell are you and what were you doing in my wagon?"

"My name's Davey Corliss. Last night after the show I heard some of the circus people talking about how they're heading for California. I made up my mind to join the circus and go to California."

"Where you from?"

"McAlester."

"How old are you, boy?"

"Fifteen, going on sixteen," Davey responded defiantly as he got to his feet. "But I'm big enough and strong enough to do the work of a man twice my age."

"You are, are you? Well, you'd best start walking back home right now so's you can start looking for work."

"I'm staying," Davey stated flatly and with no hesitation. "I told you I'm bent on joining the circus."

"Bent, are you? You'll be busted if you don't start walking east right now. Busted by me."

"I'm pretty good with my fists," Davey announced, a warning.

A man yelled suddenly, the sound coming from the west and echoing from the surrounding hills that rose in that direction.

Cimarron heard the alarm that had been in the man's voice, and when the yell came a second time, he spun around, raced around the wagon, and leaped up onto its seat. Releasing the brake, he yelled, *"Gee!"* and moved his team out, using the reins to send them into a gallop as he hurried to catch up with the cage train.

When he finally did reach it, he found that it had joined the baggage train, which was halted near the top of a high sandstone hill.

"What's wrong?" he yelled to one of the elephant keepers.

"We lost a wagon," the man yelled back. "It went over the side of that cliff over there."

Cimarron got down from the wagon and went to where a crowd of men and women were clustered. When he reached them, he too peered down into the ravine where a shattered wagon surrounded by baggage and other debris lay. Among the debris, he saw at once in the light of a flickering torch someone in the crowd was holding up, lay a motionless man, a man he immediately recognized as the cowboy who had ridden hell-for-leather after the Indians in the concluding act of the circus as he sought to rescue the screaming woman in the Conestoga wagon.

"There *wasn't* any torch!" a man cried from the crowd in answer to someone's question. "I was right behind Denton and I would have seen it if there had been one."

"But there must have been a torch!" a woman declared in a strained voice. "There would have had to be one to mark this cliff so that no one would have an accident here."

"Well, there wasn't any torch, but there sure as hell was an accident," a man muttered solemnly.

"He's dead!" a man who had climbed down into the ravine called up to the anxious crowd. "Denton's dead!"

Cimarron began to climb down the crumbling side of the

ravine, slipping and sliding as he did so because his boots found no firm footholds, intending to help the man below him bring up the body of the dead Denton, who was, he thought with regret, through kicking sawdust forever.

5

Halfway down the side of the sloping cliff, Cimarron almost lost his balance. He reached out and seized the twisted trunk of a scrub oak to halt his slide, and then, as he struggled to get a foothold, he caught movement out of the corner of his eye just beyond the oak he was clutching.

In the little light that spilled down the slope from the torches that had been lighted high above him, he was able to make out the figure of a man hunched beneath a thick outcropping of shale that jutted out from the side of the slope.

"Denton's down there," he told the faceless figure, which had its back to him. "He's dead. We could use some help in getting him up to the ridge."

When the figure didn't move—seemed, in fact, to shrink against the side of the slope—Cimarron's eyes narrowed. What's he doing down here, he asked himself, if he's not on his way down to Denton? Did he get down this far only to find his feet froze up on him? Did he lose his nerve?

"You stuck?" Cimarron called out, and was surprised to see whoever it was he had addressed move out from beneath the ledge and go scrambling horizontally across the slope. It's a man, sure enough, he thought as he caught a glimpse of the large hands and barrel-broad shoulders of the figure from beneath whose feet loose rocks and shattered shale slid down to the bottom of the ravine.

The man suddenly halted and Cimarron saw why he had

done so. The side of the cliff just ahead of him jutted out sharply, barring any further progress.

Cimarron, still holding tightly to the trunk of the scrub oak, saw the man turn and start to scramble up the side of the slope. As torchlight from above briefly illuminated his features, Cimarron recognized Crocker, the ticket seller Simpson had fired the day before.

Cimarron let go of the oak and went after Crocker, his body hugging the slope and his hands seizing jutting sandstone formations as he hoped and almost prayed that they wouldn't give way on him. As he made his way closer to his quarry, he remembered the man up on the ridge who had claimed that there had been no torch placed to warn of the precipitous passage. I'll bet dollars to doughnuts, he thought, that there was a torch and that bastard Crocker just ahead of me got his hands on it and put it out. He's got no good reason to be out here now that he's no longer with the show. No, he has got a reason, Cimarron quickly corrected himself. He told Simpson he'd get even and it looks to me like he tried to.

As he reached a position directly below the still-scrambling Crocker, Cimarron stretched and seized the man's ankle in one hand. "Hold it, Crocker. You and me, we're going up together."

Crocker kicked wildly in an effort to break Cimarron's grip, but Cimmaron held on and eased up the slope for a distance of several inches, stiffening as a rock suddenly gave way beneath his boots and he had to move fast to maintain his position. He eased up again, moving more gingerly, still gripping Crocker's ankle.

But then Crocker, clinging to the rotting trunk of an aspen that had died young, turned slightly, tore a piece of shale from the slope, and threw it down toward Cimarron.

Cimarron, when the missile struck his cheek, hunched his shoulders, lowered his head, and held on to Crocker's ankle. He eased himself farther up the slope and then let go of Crocker's ankle. Instead, he seized the man's belt, barely aware of the torchlight that was faintly visible above his former position some distance away or of the man who was slowly climbing the slope with Denton's body slung over one shoulder.

Crocker reached down and slammed a fist against the side of Cimarron's head. Cimarron swore and lunged upward.

A mistake. Because as he did so, he lost his footing, and still holding tightly to Crocker's belt, he began to slide down the side of the slope dragging Crocker, who was now screaming, with him.

Both men hit the ground hard and rolled over, dust and shards of shale and sandstone showering down around them. Cimarron was the first to get to his feet, and as Crocker rose seconds later, he drew his .44 and said, "Stay put or I'll let light through you."

"Don't shoot," Crocker said nervously. "I got no gun and I don't want to die."

"You're responsible for that wagon going over the side, aren't you?"

When Crocker said nothing, Cimarron cocked his Colt.

"Yes," Crocker cried, his eyes widening in fear. "I watched which way the baggage train was heading and I went on ahead of it until I came to that ridge up there. When the scout came along, he torched it. Once he'd gone, I put out the torch, but then I lost my footing and went over the side. Before I could get back up, I heard the baggage train coming so I hid under that outcropping back there where you first spotted me. Are you going to shoot me?"

"You caused the death of a man. Don't you figure I ought to?"

"I had a right to pay Simpson back for what he did to me."

"You didn't pay Simpson back," Cimarron snapped. "It wasn't Simpson you killed on account of what you did tonight. What kind of fool are you, Crocker, that you'd go and make another man pay for a wrong you think somebody else did you? I have half a notion to shoot you in both knees and leave you down here to die."

"No, don't! Don't do that! Please, don't do that!"

"Start climbing, Crocker. Nice and slow and easylike. I'll be right behind you all the way up to the top."

Cimarron stepped back to allow Crocker to pass him, and as Crocker did so, he stumbled and fell flat against the slope.

"That's a bad beginning, Crocker. You—"

Crocker's hand darted inside his shirt, and when it emerged, it held a long-bladed knife. He lunged at Cimarron, coming in at a crouch, and then, rising, he slashed downward.

As Crocker's knife sliced through the flesh on the back of his right hand and he dropped his gun, Cimarron swore and said, "Why, you sneaky son of a bitch you!"

Crocker laughed. "Had this tucked away in a sheath strapped to my chest. Figured it might come in handy someday. Looks like it has. No, lawman, don't go for your gun or I'll gut you!"

Cimarron, who had been stopped in the act of trying to retrieve his gun, straightened and stood facing Crocker, his gaze shifted from Crocker's wild eyes to the knife in the man's hand.

After Crocker had picked up Cimarron's gun and thrown it far up the ravine, he sprang, his right arm raised as he brandished his knife, at Cimarron, whose left arm shot out and swiftly seized Crocker's right wrist. He rotated his body to the left and at the same time swung his right leg behind Crocker's right leg and threw the man to the ground. He bent down and pulled his bowie knife from his boot, and as Crocker got to his feet fast, he was ready for him.

The two men, crouching, faced each other, and then Crocker moved slightly to the right, Cimarron to the left. They circled each other as blood from Cimarron's right hand oozed down to darken the hilt of his knife. Crocker took a swift swipe at Cimarron, his knife hand moving from right to left, but Cimarron merely leaned backward and the only casualty of the blade was the air through which it had sliced.

When Crocker failed to follow through with a left-to-right

slash, Cimarron grabbed his firearm with his left hand and held it high above the man's head. "Drop it, Crocker."

Crocker held on to his knife. He hooked his right foot behind Cimarron's right knee and jerked it forwad, sending Cimarron crashing to the ground.

As Cimarron scrambled to his knees and was about to rise, Crocker lashed out with one booted foot and kicked him, sending Cimarron toppling over backward.

Crocker bent over and his knife hand came down.

Cimarron rolled to the left out of the blade's way, and Crocker's knife buried itself in the ground. Cimarron was up, and before Crocker could pull his knife from the ground, he seized the man by the shirt, yanked him to his feet, and savagely pressed the blade of his knife into the small of Crocker's back, drawing blood.

Crocker broke free, leaving a torn piece of his shirt in Cimarron's left hand. He turned and raised his knife. As his hand came down, Cimarron dropped the scrap of Crocker's shirt. He seized Crocker's wrist and twisted it violently. As Crocker howled in pain but held on to his knife, Cimarron, rage roaring through him, muttered, "Had enough, Crocker?"

Crocker howled louder as Cimarron twisted his wrist a second time. Still he did not drop his knife. Cimarron released him and plunged his knife into the man's left bicep. Crocker screamed in pain, but as Cimarron withdrew his knife, Crocker turned and thrust, his blade glancing off Cimarron's ribs and leaving a thin bloody trail to mark its passing.

Cimarron, unbalanced by the blow, struggled to stay on his feet, and as he did so, Crocker suddenly went racing away from him. Cimarron set out after him and he had almost reached him when Crocker dropped his knife and picked up Cimarron's gun from the spot where it had landed when he had thrown it earlier. He thumbed back the hammer.

Cimarron lunged forward and booted the gun from Crocker's hand. It fired an instant before it flew from Crocker's hand, the bullet whining harmlessly away to strike the slope behind Cimarron.

Crocker retrieved his knife and rose, stepping swiftly aside as Cimarron dived toward him. He slashed at Cimarron's face and missed his target only because Cimarron drew back in time. Then, Cimarron, seized by an almost maniacal fury, brought the heavy hilt of his bowie up to crack against Crocker's lower jaw. He heard bone shatter. "Quit, Crocker," he commanded. "Now!"

But Crocker wouldn't quit. With his broken lower jaw hanging slack and useless and his knees bent so that he was nearly two feet shorter than Cimarron, who loomed over him, he brought his knife hand up in an outward and then upward arc.

Cimarron's buttocks shot out behind him as he bent his body so that its upper half was almost parallel to the ground. Crocker's intended target—his groin—remained unharmed. As Crocker's arm continued its upward swing, Cimarron threw up his left arm and knocked Crocker's arm to the side. He lunged forward and his knife plunged into Crocker's gut, his fist thudding against Crocker's body as his blade buried itself inside the man.

Crocker gagged as blood spurted from his body and Cimarron's right hand ripped upward and then around and back down again to empty Crocker's gut of a mass of looped intestines and several bloodied organs.

As Cimarron withdrew his knife and stood panting, his boots planted far apart, Crocker dropped his knife and looked down in wide-eyed horror at what had happened to him. His lips quivered as his hands moved slowly toward his midsection. Cimarron stood his ground and watched as Crocker desperately tried to force the parts of himself that had escaped the prison of his body back into their proper places. He failed to do so. Air eased out of his mouth, which was open because of his dangling broken jaw, and he crumpled to the ground to lie there writhing and trying to speak but unable to do so.

His eyes were on the sky he could no longer see because

Cimarron's blade had summoned Death, and Death had come to claim Crocker, whose bleeding had stopped at the terrible touch of Death's hard hand.

Cimarron wiped the sweat from his forehead with the back of his hand. He bent down and wiped his blade clean on a tuft of thick grass and then returned it to his right boot. He retrieved his revolver, and after wiping the back of his bloody right hand on his jeans, he thumbed a cartridge out of its loop on his gun belt and eased it into the empty cylinder of his gun. Then, tilting his hat back on his head so that he could more easily see the top of the slope, he began to climb toward it without giving Crocker's corpse another glance.

A sharp pain seared his upper torso as he climbed, the result of the long but shallow wound Crocker had inflicted on his rib cage. He made slow and dusty progress as he mounted, slid back, climbed again toward the flickering torches that seemed to have replaced the stars in the cloudy sky above him. At last, he heaved himself up and over the edge of the rimrock and he lay there for a moment, his breathing ragged as a result of both the fight in the ravine below and the strain of his difficult ascent.

"You killed him," a woman accused.

Cimarron, his eyes squeezed shut, opened them and raised his head. He placed his palms flat on the ground, raised his body, and looked up at Lucinda. His head dropped and hung down for a moment before he looked up at her again.

"You ripped him open," she breathed.

"I did. Almost from gut to gullet."

"Cimarron!" Babe Folsom, huge arms shoving people out of her way, came hurrying toward him. "Are you hurt? Where are you hurt?" She flopped on the ground in front of him, her dress fluttering down around her. She took his face between her big hands and looked into his eyes. "I thought he was going to kill you."

"I'm glad he didn't, Babe, but the fact of the matter is he did come too close for this man's comfort."

Cimarron became aware of the crowd surrounding him and

84

Babe. Faces, most of which he didn't recognize, peered down at him, all of them tense and some of them showing traces of fear. What are they afraid of? he asked himself. Me?

"Come on, Cimarron," Babe said. "I'll help you back to your wagon."

"Who was that man?" asked Gunther as he stepped out of the crowd. "We couldn't see his face clearly from up here."

"Crocker. Simpson fired him yesterday. He's the one who caused the accident. He put out the torch the scout set up to guide us."

"We saw him try to kill you," Babe said as she tried to get up.

"We saw *you* kill *him*," Lucinda added, a strange light in her eyes.

From the torches? Cimarron stood up and then bent down to help Babe, who was unable to regain her feet unassisted. Once on her feet, she took his arm.

"We'll go to your wagon. Tinker," she called out to the clown Lucinda had introduced to Cimarron the day he had arrived on the lot in McAlester. "You go get the first-aid box and bring it to Cimarron's wagon." Turning anxious eyes on Cimarron, she asked, "Will you be able to drive it?"

"Me? My wagon? Sure."

"I'll spell him," Davey Corliss said from behind Cimarron.

"You're a cute little fellow," Babe cried, her eyes blinking at Corliss. "But who are you and how come you're here when you don't look old enough to be up past midnight or even nine o'clock, for that matter?"

"My name is Davey Corliss and I've come to join the circus."

"You know this boy?" Babe asked Cimarron.

"I know him. Made his acquaintance a little bit ago. Thought I'd sent him packing, but it appears I failed to do so."

"You take him to the wagon, miss," Davey directed Babe. "I'll drive it once we get going again."

"Miss," Babe repeated, shaking her head. "How I hate that word, but the way things are with me—the way I *am*—

why, I expect I'll be hearing that word when I finally land in the halls of hell."

She draped Cimarron's left arm over her shoulders and began to walk slowly toward his wagon. "You think you can make it?"

Cimarron, in no need of physical support, nevertheless answered, "I reckon I can, Babe. With your help, that is."

Babe beamed at him, her face a round rosy ball in the torchlit night, which was becoming noisy as the circus prepared to move out again.

"It's a damn shame about Denton," Babe remarked, her hot left hand gripping Cimarron's left wrist. "With him dead, the gaffer will have his hands full finding somebody to replace him in the show's finale."

"One of the boys who's playing an Indian now could join the other side and play Denton's cowboy part," Cimarron suggested.

"And have just *two* Indians chasing the Conestoga? That wouldn't do. Why, we used to have *four* Indians, but one of them married a girl in a town back east and quit the show. And everybody else is already working to take the show down when that act's on so there's no one I can think of to take Denton's place in the act." Babe suddenly halted.

"What's the matter?"

"I was watching you on that horse of yours when you rode onto the lot yesterday. You looked to me like a cowboy the way you sat so tall in the saddle and rode so fast but real sure and steady."

"Now, hold on, Babe. I'm not about to take Denton's place in the show. I'd make a damn fool of myself in front of all those people."

"Mr. Simpson," Babe called out, and when she had Simpson's attention, she beckoned and he came up to her. "Mr. Simpson, Cimarron is the man to take Denton's place in the last act. He can ride like the wind."

"Splendid," Simpson crowed. "I should have thought of

you as a replacement right away, Cimarron, but I've been upset. The accident . . ."

"Mr. Simpson, now, you listen to me a minute," Cimarron began, but Babe interrupted him by saying, "Think about it, Cimarron. There you are on your big horse. The Indians are yelling. They're about to burn the wagon and do God only knows what to that poor helpless woman in it. But you ride after them, your guns firing, your face shining like a brave knight of olden times. You drive the red devils off and then you—"

"No, Babe."

"The women in the audience," Babe continued, undaunted, "will swoon at the mere sight of you."

"You're not an ugly man, Cimarron," Simpson interjected slyly after Babe had given him a surreptitious wink.

"When they see you—so muscled and manly—they'll all fall ass over tin cup in love with you, Cimarron," Babe insisted. "And when they take to their beds after the show's over, they'll dream of you riding *them*, not that horse of yours."

Simpson guffawed.

Cimarron licked his lips in anticipation of fulfilling the fantasy Babe was weaving for his benefit and, he knew, for the benefit of the circus as well. He saw the women in the seats watching him as he rode after the counterfeit Indians chasing the wagon. He felt their yearning eyes on him. He imagined some of them—the ones without husbands or scruples—putting their hot hands on him, on his— Some of them might want to do just that, he thought, feeling a pleasant tension growing in his groin. Maybe some of them would do it if he played his cards right after the show.

"Fifteen dollars a week," Simpson said.

"Sounds fine to me," Cimarron said.

"Then we have a deal. You can rehearse the act in the morning after you've been patched up and had a chance to rest."

As Simpson left them, Cimarron and Babe continued walking toward his wagon and Cimarron found himself looking forward to the rehearsal in the morning.

Once inside his wagon, Cimarron sat down on his board bunk, and as Babe lit the lamp, he obeyed and stripped off his shirt.

She stuck her head out the door of the wagon and shouted, "Tinker!"

When the man came running with the bulky first-aid box in his hands, she took it from him and then ordered him to heat some water and bring that too, which he promptly did. He stood in the doorway watching as Babe washed Cimarron's wounded hand and ribs and then swabbed antiseptic on them.

"You didn't so much as flinch," Tinker commented, shaking his head in surprise. "And that stuff sure does sting."

"Knives sting worse," Cimarron remarked. "When you've been cut up and shot as many times as I've been, it takes more than this stuff to make you flinch."

"Thanks for what you did for us tonight," Tinker said. "That Crocker was a no-good bastard from the word go."

"He was," Babe agreed as she bandaged Cimarron's ribs and hand. "We're well rid of him."

Cimarron felt her hand caress his chest as she pretended to tighten the bandage on his side. "You should've been a nurse, Babe. You've got a real soft touch."

"And a softer heart for all the good it does me," Babe responded, a trace of bitterness in her tone.

"Don't you go despairing, Babe," Tinker said. "One of these days you'll meet a man who dotes on big bundles of joy like you."

"You never gave me a tumble, Tinker."

"One of these days maybe I will." Tinker ducked as Babe threw a pillow at him and then he disappeared.

"Those two—Tinker and Matt Ledman," Babe said. "I wouldn't mind taking on the pair of them at one time. I'd have to, because they stick that close to each other. They're as close as two peas in a pod."

Ramona Bertolini appeared in the doorway of the wagon, a

lantern in her hand. "Cimarron, is there anything I can do for you?"

"Step on in, Ramona," Cimarron said, and caught the flash of anger in Babe's eyes as Ramona climbed into the wagon and set her lantern down on the floor.

"Well, two's company, as they say," Babe remarked and, carrying the first-aid box, lumbered out of the wagon.

Ramona sat down in the only chair in the wagon and her eyes went to the bandages on Cimarron's body.

"Nice of you to come by to see if I was still among the living, Ramona." He stood up and unstrapped his gun rig and placed it on the floor before sitting down again.

"I knew you were alive," Ramona said softly. "I saw what happened. That isn't why I came."

Cimarron rose and started to close the door. Just before he shut it, he caught a glimpse of Gunther standing in the darkness outside as wagons and carts rumbled past him. He turned and, leaning back against the closed door, his feet angled outward so that his legs formed an inverted V, asked, "Why did you come?"

Instead of answering, Ramona rose to her feet. She hesitated a moment and then approached him. She placed her hands on his cheeks and pulled his head down toward her. She kissed him and then drew back, looking up into his eyes. "Does that answer your question?"

"You came for a kiss?"

"For this too," she whispered, her hand coming to rest between his legs.

"Well, now, don't you know how to make a man glad!" Cimarron embraced her, her body stiff against his stiffening shaft. She's too damned skittish, he thought. She needs to relax and ride along easy with what's about to happen. He kissed her, parting her teeth with his tongue, encountering resistance at first, and then, if not exactly surrender, at least acceptance.

He ran his hands up and down her spine, and as the wagon

lurched and pulled out, he took her hand and led her to his bunk.

Ramona sat down on its edge and remained motionless as he began to unfasten the row of buttons that ran from her throat to her slim waist. She neither moved nor looked up at him as he slipped her dress down over her shoulders, reached behind her, and loosened her stays to bare her breasts.

Small but firm, they gleamed creamy in the lantern's light. He took them in his hands and squeezed them gently. He spread her legs and knelt between them, taking her right breast in his mouth, teasing her nipple with his tongue. Then he repeated what he had done with her left breast before rising and beginning to unbutton his jeans, which covered the bulge lying against his thigh, the result of his lust for Ramona that was storming within him.

"No."

Ramona had spoken the word so softly that Cimarron had barely heard it. Ignoring her denial, he sat down on the bunk beside her and was about to pull off his boots, his erection throbbing, when she suddenly said, "I can't do it. I wanted to do it. I told myself I should do it. I have as much right to enjoy myself as anyone, Gunther von Kleist included. He has no qualms about who he takes to bed. Why should I have any?"

Cimarron groaned as he began to understand.

"I made sure he saw me come in here."

"You set out tonight to make Gunther jealous, is that it?"

"Yes, I did. But now—I can't. I'm sorry, Cimarron. I shouldn't have tried to use you."

"Why don't you just go ahead and use me, honey? You're here. I'm here. We've got the rest of the night straight ahead of us. I'm willing to let you use me any which way you want." He reached for her, but she pulled away from him.

"No, it's no good. You're a very attractive man, Cimarron. I suspect you know that. But it's Gunther I really want. I love him. But he—he—"

"Loves Lucinda."

"Damn her to hell!" Ramona cried furiously. She hastily pulled her dress up over her shoulders, and after frantically buttoning it, she picked up her lantern and ran for the door. She opened it, leaped down to the ground, and vanished into the night.

Cimarron, thoroughly frustrated, stared after her for a moment and then got up and booted the door shut. He sat down on the bunk again and, after giving a resigned sigh, leaned back against the wall of the wagon. He firmly gripped his upright flesh and set about the solitary and, for him, ultimately unrewarding task of seeking the release Ramona had promised and then denied him.

6

The rising sun streaked the skyful of low-riding white clouds
with gold the next morning as Cimarron, with Davey seated
beside him, drove his wagon westward.

"Maybe you're making a mistake, Davey," Cimarron said
at last, shattering the silence that had lain between them for
the past mile. "The circus may not be where you belong."

"Maybe it's not," Davey said, surprising Cimarron and
causing him to give the boy a sidelong glance. "But I got no
single other place where I belong."

"No folks?"

"There's just Pa and he don't care about nothing but where
his next bottle of red-eye's coming from."

"You pa drinks a bit?"

"Night and day."

"Most men like a drink now and then. I do."

"Pa likes a few too many. That's why he put me out to
hire—for the money he's too drunk most of the time to earn
for himself even if anybody would hire him, which they
won't because everybody in McAlester and for miles around
knows about his habit."

"If you've got a job back in McAlester, you ought not to
let loose of it so easy. A good job steadies a man—or a
boy."

"Pa didn't let me keep a cent of what I earned working for
Bart Sutter in that butcher shop of his. Pa took it all. He

claimed that since I got my keep from Mr. Sutter I ought to be satisfied. Well, I wasn't. Who would be, wallowing about in blood and guts and sides of pork and beef day in and day out, except for Sundays, from can-see to can't-see?"

"Your pa's still family, though, and blood ties bind tight. I reckon he'll miss you."

"What he'll miss is the money I had to turn over to him every Saturday. That, and maybe the chance to belt me from time to time when the liquor got him all riled up."

Cimarron looked up at the sky in which the clouds were no longer gold but white now, and then at the horizon in the distance.

"The last time he unlooped that belt of his—that was only yesterday," Davey continued, "I got it away from him and—I used it on *him*. Then I ran and now I'm here and it's here I intend to stay."

The figure of a man suddenly appeared on the horizon, a giant who loomed larger than life, and Cimarron tried to look away from the man who was his own father, but he found he couldn't. Stern of visage, Cimarron's father admonished his son, and when his words had no effect, he slid his leather belt from its loops and Cimarron—the boy he had been—felt that belt slash his shoulders, then his back, and finally his buttocks.

". . . my pa's not really a mean man," Davey was saying, a note of wistfulness in his soft voice. "It's the booze that makes him mean. He gets to needing somebody to hurt and I was most always there when the mean mood was on him."

Cimarron saw himself fleeing the home place as he had done so many years ago while the man towering above the horizon shook a finger at him in an anger that was tinged with despair. He saw himself growing up in saloons and brothels and boardinghouses as he worked in sawmills and on ranches, as a swamper in a saloon in Ogden, Utah, and as a three-card monte gambler on a Mississippi riverboat.

". . . and I'm not ever going back to McAlester," Davey stated firmly.

Cimarron heard the defiant echo of himself vowing, in his

forever lost and distant past, never to return to the home place in central Texas, and as Davey beside him dreamed aloud of the cities he would soon see and of California waiting to welcome him beyond the far mountains, Cimarron remembered his own young dreaming, which had turned at last into bitter years served in a Denver jail for having murdered a cardsharp.

As the sky above him brightened, his thoughts darkened and he was once again riding with the hard cases he had joined following his release from jail. Storm clouds gathered in his mind as he saw himself kneeling in front of the iron safe in the bank that he and the other outlaws were robbing in the Texas Panhandle, as he heard one of his companions shout a warning, as he saw himself turn and get off a fast shot that dropped the sheriff who had been silhouetted, the sun behind him, in the doorway of the bank.

Up and running, Cimarron was past the sheriff, having given the dead man only the briefest of glances . . .

He halted. Looked back and down. And thought he too was about to die where he stood stricken, his boots rooted to the wooden floor, his eyes on his father, whom he had just shot and killed and who now was staring up at him through empty eyes.

He asked his questions and received his answers from the terrified clerks and patrons in the bank. The sheriff had come to their town, they told him, after the death of his wife. He was a good and reliable man, they said, and in time, at their request, he had become their sheriff.

Cimarron ran from the bank, the answers he had received resounding in his ears. He tossed the moneybags he was carrying to one of the other outlaws who was already mounted and ready to ride, leaped into his saddle, and rode away. Alone.

And alone he had been ever since, even when surrounded by men in towns or on long-since-forgotten trails or when lying in the arms of women who had no faces in towns that had no names.

"So there's no use in trying to talk me into going back," Davey stated flatly.

"I reckon there's not," Cimarron said as his father, almost blotting out the world in the west now, pointed an accusing finger at him and spoke an indictment of him that was made all the more terrible because it had been spoken in a voice soft with regret and shattered by pain that was far more than merely physical—pain that derived, Cimarron knew, from having tried his very best only to find that his best was never good enough or even acceptable insofar as his son was concerned.

"Maybe you think I'm a quitter," Davey said defensively, "because I cut and ran. But you don't know what it was like living the way I was, what with Pa's beatings and—"

"Maybe I do know," Cimarron said as the dead man he still dreaded faded away to become a part of the blue sky and his own tormented mind.

Davey gave him a questioning glance, which he ignored.

"Sometimes, Davey, quitting's all a man can do. It's not always a bad thing to do."

"Most folks look down on it."

"An outlaw can quit killing," Cimarron commented without acknowledging the truth of Davey's remark but, rather, trying to point out to the boy that most folks, in his opinion, himself very much included, had a lot left to learn in their lives. "A man can quit a bad place and set out to find himself a good one. Or at least a better one."

"Is that what you did?" Davey paused a moment before hesitantly asking, "You were an outlaw and you quit killing? Is that what you're telling me? That after you quit riding the owl-hoot trail you went hunting for some place good?"

"I'm not telling you nothing about me. I'm just trying to speak the truth as I see it, only maybe you don't agree with me."

"Oh, I agree with you, all right. It's just that you took me by surprise. You just don't seem to think the way most folks do."

"I reckon that's a fact."

"How come folks call you Cimarron? You got a real name?"

Cimarron felt anger awakening within him and he tried to fight it down. Why the hell do I have to talk so much? he asked himself. And to a still-wet-behind-the-ears kid at that? He knew why. Davey, like a conjuror of unwitting skill, had spoken, and his words had summoned the memory of the boy Cimarron had been to once again do battle with the ghost of the father he had murdered; and the result had been that he had reached out to try to help Davey, an act that had resulted in Davey's sensing correctly the dark history they shared.

"I like it," Davey said.

"You like what?"

"Your name. Cimarron. It's a name with a real ring to it. I wish I had one like it."

The anger abruptly died within Cimarron. He knew what Davey was trying to tell him. Not just that the boy liked his name but that he liked him. Probably because he's been smart enough to guess that I've traveled the same trail he happens to be on at the moment. Or maybe because I held some hope out to him instead of acting like a circuit preacher pleading with one of the drags to come up the aisle and be saved.

"You figure they'll let me stay with the circus, Cimarron? If they don't, I haven't a notion as to what to do next. I've only got thirty-five cents in my jeans and a hunger in my belly that feels like it's going to bust me wide open so it can get out and find some food."

"See there? Up there just this side of the horizon? That's a town called Paradise up there on Mustang Creek, though why it's called that I guess I'll never know, since it's a hell-on-the-border kind of town like a whole lot of others here in the Territory. When we get there and get the show set up, I'll talk to Mr. Simpson. He ought to be able to find something to keep you busy."

"What if it turns out he won't let me stay on and work?"

"Well, now, there's a couple of answers to that question,

Davey. The first one that comes to mind is you could put down stakes in Paradise and be—well, maybe you could be a three-card monte dealer. I was one once. I could teach you the tricks of the trade."

"I'm not keen on gambling. I'd rather stay with the circus, if they'll let me."

"Tell you what. If the gaffer can't find work for you, I'll make you my assistant at least till we reach the Texas border."

"What would I be assisting you at?"

"You don't know that I'm a deputy United States marshal?" When Davey shook his head, Cimarron said, "I am, and though you're too young for me to commission as a deputy, which I could do if you were old enough, I don't see why you couldn't be my assistant deputy United States marshal."

"You got the power, have you, to make me that?"

"Why, sure I have," Cimarron replied, well aware that there was no such position associated with the Court for the Western District of Arkansas.

"I guess being your assistant deputy would be better than being a gambler," Davey mused. "Pa, he'd call gambling a sin."

The wrathful ghost of his father roared suddenly in Cimarron's mind as he spoke now in death, as he had so often done in life, of repentance and redemption, of sin and the terrible and eternal pain of hell fire. Cimarron, banishing the wraith, remarked, "Sin's a lot like an ingredient in a woman's recipe for one of her tastiest dishes. It adds some spice to a man's life."

Davey blushed.

Cimarron grinned and, after poking Davey in the ribs, gave the boy a wicked wink.

Both of them began to laugh and they were both still laughing later as the circus train halted on the eastern outskirts of Paradise.

As the roustabouts, who had been sleeping in wagons during the night, climbed out of them rubbing their eyes, and as yawning performers began to appear, Cimarron parked his wagon in an out-of-the-way spot. Then, beckoning to Davey, he moved through the chaotic crowd in search of Mr. Simpson.

He found the gaffer sitting sleepily on the steps of his wagon. "Mr. Simpson, this here stray I happened upon back along the trail is looking for work. I'm hoping you'll give him some."

"What can you do, son?" Simpson asked.

"Most anything at all that needs doing, sir," Davey answered enthusiastically.

"You look to be on the frail side," Simpson remarked skeptically.

"Oh, I'm not at all frail, sir. I'm as strong as a grain-fed ox. Every boy where I went to school refused to arm-wrassle with me because I always won."

Simpson, smiling, said, "See the boss hostler over there." He pointed the man out to Davey. "Tell Scott I put you on the payroll. You'll earn seventy-five cents a day and get your grub in the cook tent. Now, we'll have to find quarters for you. Perhaps—"

"He's bunking with me, Mr. Simpson," Cimarron interjected.

"Thanks, Cimarron," Davey cried. "Hey, thanks a whole lot. Thank you too, Mr. Simpson. I appreciate what you've done for me and I swear you won't be sorry. I'll work hard, I will. I promise!"

Davey raced across the lot and spoke to the boss hostler. A moment later he joined the other roustabouts, who were pulling on the thick rope to raise the big top as they chanted, "Heave it, weave it, shake it, take it, break it, make it, move along!"

"The boy's got sand," Cimarron commented. "Looks like you've hired yourself a real hard worker, Mr. Simpson."

"You'd better rehearse your part in the roper act," Simpson suggested. "There's Matt Ledman standing over near the candy butcher's stand. He'll tell you what you have to do."

Cimarron left Simpson, and when he reached Ledman, he introduced himself to the unsmiling man, who ignored his outthrust hand.

Ledman spat a stream of tobacco juice and remarked laconically, "Tinker told me about you. Simpson told me you're taking Denton's place in the roper act."

"Why do you people call it a 'roper act'?"

"That's circus lingo. Roper means cowboy. You want to run through the routine so you can get the hang of it?"

When Cimarron agreed to do so, Ledman rounded up the men who played the parts of the Indians in the act and the female passenger in the stagecoach and then, after Cimarron had gotten his horse, they proceeded to rehearse the act that closed each night's show.

"Maybe we can add a trick or two to make this thing a bit more interesting," Cimarron suggested after the second run-through. "Now, I mean no offense to you fellows. The act's fine as it stands. But—well, here's the sort of thing I had in mind."

"One or more of us is liable to break our necks trying stunts like that," Ledman commented when Cimarron had finished outlining his suggestions for livening up the act.

"But if we can do what this roper's proposing we do," one of the Indians declared gleefully, "we'll really give the marks a thrill for their money."

"You game, miss?" Cimarron asked the woman who played the part of the passenger in the wagon, and when she smiled and nodded, he and the others ran through the act a third time—doing it his way—and then Ledman pointed to the flag that was rising above the cook tent. "Time to quit and eat, boys! Let's go!"

Cimarron dismounted and followed the others, who were eagerly heading toward the cook tent.

That night Cimarron stood just to the left of the entrance to the big top, holding his horse's reins in his hand and listening to the music that accompanied Lucinda Powell's *haute école* performance. Behind him stood the Conestoga wagon and in it sat the woman who would soon be rescued from the marauding Indians. On either side of the wagon the three

Indians wearing feathered headdresses sat their horses, smoking cigars and gossiping among themselves.

Ledman, who was on the wagon seat, said, "Our cue's coming up. You all set, roper?"

"I'm set," Cimarron said as the audience inside the tent burst into loud applause that was sprinkled with rowdy cheers from several men.

Lucinda rode out of the big top, and as she gave Cimarron a smile, the Conestoga went rolling into the tent; then, a moment later, war whooping and brandishing their lances and painted canvas shields, the Indians went after the wagon.

Lucinda rode over to Cimarron. She raised her hand, kissed the tips of her fingers, and then pressed them against his cheek. "That's for luck."

"I'll need it," he said. "I've never been in any kind of show before and I'm feeling about as nervy as a steer just before a thunderstorm strikes." He grabbed his lariat, spurred his horse, and rode out after the three Indians.

As he galloped into view, a cheer went up from the audience. The audience cheered more wildly and many rose to their feet as he swung a wide loop that he dropped around the Indian closest to him. He jerked the man from his mount and then snapped his lariat to loosen it. As it flew free, the Indian hit the tanbark and rolled over, pretending to have been stunned into unconsciousness.

The woman inside the wagon screamed.

Whirling the lariat above his head, Cimarron threw an overhead toss, and his rope settled around the neck of an Indian's horse, halting it. He drew his revolver and, brandishing it in a menacing manner, forced the Indian to leap from his horse and go running out of the tent, causing more cheers and a few "hurrahs" to rise from the audience.

He abandoned his lariat and rode after the remaining Indian. But the man, following the suggestion Cimarron had made to him during their rehearsal, threw his lance. Cimarron swerved to one side so that the lance landed harmlessly in the tanbark. He galloped toward the wagon at the end of the hippodrome track and, when he reached it, stood up in his saddle, grabbed the luggage boot with both hands, and hauled himself up onto the wagon seat. He ripped the reins from Ledman's hands and turned the wagon as the woman inside it continued screaming at the top of her voice and the audience continued cheering wildly.

He turned the team and sent them galloping back the way they had come, causing the remaining Indian to let out a cry of alarm as the wagon began to bear down upon him. As the Indian retrieved and raised his lance, Cimarron holstered his Colt, reached down into the luggage boot, and came up with the horse whip that he had placed there earlier. He snapped the whip once and ripped the lance out of the Indian's hand. He swiftly snapped the whip again and the Indian's shield was torn from his hand. He dropped the whip and drew his gun. He fired a shot that was deliberately aimed high above the head of the Indian, who quickly turned his horse and went galloping away from the wagon, which was rapidly bearing down on him, until he was out of the tent.

A moment later, to thunderous applause, Cimarron drove the wagon out of the tent.

"You were marvelous," Lucinda called up to him as he halted the team and put on the brake. "Simply marvelous!"

"You stayed to watch, did you?"

"And I'm glad I did, Cimarron. You're an asset to the show in more ways than one. You're not only our protector but a splendid performer as well."

As the band in the tent began to play "The Star-Spangled Banner," Cimarron climbed down from the wagon seat and said, "It kind of tickled me to hear all those folks cheering me on the way they did. They sure did seem to be rooting for me all the way down the line."

"Oh, they were," Lucinda cried. "Wasn't he wonderful, Matt?"

Ledman grunted something unintelligible and drove away.

"You were heroic, Cimarron, that's what you were. There's just no other word to describe your performance."

"That's the first time I ever performed like that. Though there are other kinds of performances I've gotten to be pretty good at." He put his arm around her waist and drew her close to him.

"I've no idea what you're talking about."

"Don't you?" He leaned over and whispered in her ear, expecting either a slap or a ladylike scream.

Lucinda gave him a sly smile.

"Stop the music!"

The command had been shouted inside the tent and it was immediately repeated.

As the music came to a ragged stop, Cimarron released Lucinda and peered into the tent.

"What was that all about?" she asked. Before he could reply, she said, "Look. Those men—what are they doing to Gunther?"

Three men were dragging a furiously struggling Gunther into the ring.

Men with rifles suddenly rose from their seats in the audience and quickly took up strategic positions beneath the tent, their guns trained on the gaping circus performers who remained in the tent, the Indian Cimmaron had first unhorsed among them.

A tall, florid-faced man stood up, his eyes dark and his glance cold and deadly as he stared down at Gunther, and then let his eyes roam over the audience. Speaking in a voice that was both resonant and chilling, he said, "Let no man raise a hand to help the evildoer you see before you. My men—every one of them a member of the Brothers of Biblical Vengeance—will shoot you if you should be so rash as to attempt to lend aid and comfort to God's enemy."

He fixed his gaze on Gunther again and, pointing a bony finger at the animal trainer, declared, "I hereby notify you of the charges against you."

A hush descended on the audience.

"I, Brother Ezra, charge you with having openly demonstrated to one and all here present that you possess the awful and infernal power of witchcraft and that you did do—''

Lucinda screamed as a man seized her from behind.

Cimarron lunged to the side and made a grab for the man who was trying to drag Lucinda into the tent. He caught him by the shoulder and tried to prevent him from moving.

Four strong hands seized him from behind and held him. A moment later, his arms were painfully pinned behind his back. He could only watch as the man who had seized Lucinda dragged her into the tent and over to the spot where Gunther, an expression of disbelief on his face, stood staring up at Brother Ezra, who glowered down at him.

"You, woman," Brother Ezra bellowed at Lucinda, "also stand accused before both God and man. Like he who stands beside you, you have shown shamelessly and with a veritable air of harlotry that you too possess the evil and abominable powers of witchcraft, conjuration, enchantment, and sorcery.''

"You're insane," Lucinda cried, struggling desperately but unable to free herself from her captor.

"Of what do you dare accuse us?" Gunther roared.

Brother Ezra replied, "I accuse you of being persons of evil and depraved dispositions. I accuse you of having private conferences with the spirit of darkness so that you may gain control, unnaturally, over the dumb brutes of God's great Creation.''

Lucinda and Gunther exchanged stunned glances.

"Sinners!" thundered Brother Ezra, addressing the members of the audience. "You all know me. I have lived and worked among you for more than a year now. I have tried to lead you down the too-little-trodden path of virtue. I have exhorted you men to become Brothers of Biblical Vengeance and I have exhorted you women to join the Sisters of the Holy Light Sodality. Some of you have come to us. Many of you have not. Now, I ask you all, how have you repaid me for my efforts in your souls' behalf? With repentance for your multitude of sins? *No!* You have repaid me in this abominable fashion—by coming here, and with your dear and innocent children at your side, to this wicked occasion of sin where witches like that whore of Babylon''—Brother Ezra's arm snaked out and his finger jabbed in Lucinda's direction—''and the warlock standing so defiantly beside her, the spawn of the spirit of darkness''—Brother Ezra's finger pointed at Gunther—''both try to seduce you with unnatural acts that fly in the face of the divine order of this world we all must live virtuously and die shriven in.''

Women in the audience blushed and lowered their heads. Some of the men looked away from their accuser and pulled at their chins or ran nervous fingers between their collars and their necks.

Cimarron lifted his right foot and brought his boot down brutally on the instep of one of the men holding him. As the man let out a yelp of pain and his grip loosened, Cimarron bent down and was about to try to throw one or both of his captors over his head when a fist descended and struck the base of his skull, dropping him to his knees. He was gripped again by four hands, but he fought to remain conscious. Dimly, he realized that Brother Ezra was speaking again.

''Who among you will stand with me and the other Brothers of Biblical Vengeance? Rise up to show your allegiance to us.''

As several members of the audience got to their feet, a man shouted, his words faint in Cimarron's ears, ''You're a fanatic, Ezra Platt. This is only a circus—''

''It is Sodom,'' Brother Ezra shot back as a woman began to sing a hymn and others, both men and women, added their voices to hers.

Cimarron raised his head and saw the man who had attempted to defy Brother Ezra being pummeled by a man standing next to him.

''You all saw what they did,'' Brother Ezra ranted. ''The Babylonian whore made her horse do what no horse the good God ever breathed life into was meant to do. You saw that half-naked monster from the black pit cause wild creatures to do what only Satan rampant could permit them to do under the guidance of one of his own. Only by having let Satan know them carnally could these depraved creatures—the man as well as the woman—do what we have all seen them do."

"That horse," a woman screamed, "she bewitched it!"

"Those wild beasts," bellowed a man, "witch taught them be, sure as shootin'."

"Say you all so?" roared Brother Ezra as the white blur that was Cimarron's world began to assume for him the firm outlines of reality again.

Most members of the audience, children included, he noticed, shouted their assent to Brother Ezra's question.

"Go you peacefully to your homes, then." Brother Ezra admonished the flock he had succeeded in bringing to a frenzy that bordered on the maniacal so that it drowned out any dissenting voices that might have tried to be heard. "That witch and that warlock shall be lodged as our prisoners this night, and tomorrow, when the good God's first shaft of holy light appears in the sky, they shall be *burrrnnned!*"

As Brother Ezra's final word resounded throughout the tent and seemed to echo in the air, Cimarron lunged foward, toppling one of the men who was holding him. He sprang to his feet and swung his fist. His left uppercut caught the second of his captors below the jaw and he was about to follow up with a right cross when someone yelled, "Cimarron, look out behind you!"

Too late, he turned.

The man he had thrown brought down his fists, his fingers interlaced, and they struck the top of Cimarron's head with the force of a nine-pound sledgehammer.

He was unconscious before he struck the ground.

7

Cimarron gradually drifted up out of darkness into a world that was filled with voices babbling excitedly.

". . . we'll go in and tear the damned town apart!"

"Let's turn Paradise into perdition!"

He rose to his hands and knees from his spread-eagled, facedown position on the ground and then stiffened as his head filled with pain and seemed about to split wide open.

"He's awake," he heard someone say.

As the babbling continued, softer now, he heard his name spoken several times and caught other words—soft but determined words—"those townie bastards . . . look after our own . . . kill . . ."

"No," he said in a weak, barely audible voice. "No killing."

"But you heard what that devil incarnate said, Cimarron."

He recognized Babe's voice, and then, as he hauled himself to his feet, he saw her standing in front of him, a worried expression on her face, as she continued, "They're going to burn Gunther and Lucinda alive Cimarron. We've got to rescue them."

"Let's go," said the lemonade butcher, a hatchet clutched in his hand, as he stood grim-faced beside Babe.

Cimarron shook his head. He bent down and picked up his hat, which had fallen from his head when he was struck, and put it on. "You folks are talking killing. How many guns you got among you?"

There was a momentary silence as people gazed at one another, asked questions, shook their heads.

"None," the lemonade butcher finally said to Cimarron.

"You're wrong on that score," Tinker Sloan piped from the rear of the crowd. He pushed his way forward until he was facing Cimarron. "I've got a gun. I bought it back in Fort Smith." He smiled broadly. "To tell you the plain truth, Cimarron, I wasn't willing to trust my life and limbs to one lone deputy out here with redskins and desperadoes roaming around. I'll get it and go with you."

"No, you won't. I appreciate your offer of help, Tinker, but— Well, to put it plainly, have you ever so much as even fired that gun you say you bought?"

Tinker's smile faded. Glumly, he shook his head and then, smiling gaily again, said, "You could teach me how to use it on our way to town."

It was Cimarron's turn to shake his head.

"I've got this hatchet," the lemonade butcher said. He held it up for Cimarron to see. "We can use tent stakes as clubs."

"You saw the rifles those men belonging to Brother Ezra had. He's got more men and more rifles in reserve, no doubt. You boys wouldn't have a chance going up against all those guns. No, you all stay put right here till I get back. I was assigned to see to it that you got through the Territory safe and sound and I intend to see to it that you all do."

"But one man can't stand up to that mob of religious fanatics," Tinker protested. "I'd feel a lot better if you'd let me lend you a hand."

"Oh, let him, Cimarron," Babe pleaded. "Please let him."

"I appreciate your intentions, Tinker," Cimarron said. "It's nice to know you and the rest of the men are willing to stand by my side in this matter. But it'll be better if I handle this on my own and in my own way. Does anybody here happen to know where exactly the jail is in town?"

At first, no one answered him, but then Ramona, who was

standing behind and to one side of Babe, said, "I didn't see any jail when we paraded through town this morning. But I did see a building that had a sign on it that said, 'Justice of the Peace.' "

"That's likely as not the law in Paradise," Cimarron mused, and asked Ramona for the building's exact location, which she described to him in detail.

"You sure you can handle things on your own?" a roustabout called out skeptically to Cimarron.

"When fellows like those two who had their hands on me treat me the way they did, I turn touchy as a teased snake. I reckon I can handle things on my own."

"I'll go with you, Cimarron."

Cimarron turned to find Davey Corliss, his hands angrily fisted at his sides, standing not far away. "I'm obliged for your offer of help, boy, but like I said, I'll handle things my way and lawfullike."

"How?" Davey asked, worry and skepticism in his voice.

How? Cimarron asked himself. Now, isn't that one helluva hard question for me to answer?

A man came riding up to the crowd from the west and drew rein. "They got only one man I could see guarding the place where they took Gunther and Lucinda. I followed them and watched where they took them."

"To the justice of the peace's place?" Cimarron asked, and the man nodded. "One guard, you say—that you could see?"

The man nodded again, and Cimarron observed, "They'll likely have others staked out and about in case some of us get the notion to storm the jail."

"Cimarron," Davey said, "you could get yourself killed."

Cimarron reached out, gripped the boy's shoulder, and squeezed it. "Don't you go fretting about me getting killed. If there's any killing to be done, I promise you I won't be the one who'll be slinging hash in hell once the shooting's over and done with."

Seeing an expression of relief flood Davey's face, Cimarron silently wished that he was as sure of not getting killed as he had sounded.

"Cimarron!" Simpson cried out as he forced his way through the crowd. "I just heard what happened. I was taking a nap in my wagon and the boss hostler woke me— What are we going to do?"

"I'm riding into Paradise, Mr. Simpson, and I hope to find a way to bring Gunther and Lucinda back all hale and hearty."

"Oh, dear," Simpson wailed. "I hope you can. Cimarron, you must! They're in such terrible danger. To think that anyone in this day and age could consider burning anyone at the stake. It's barbarous. Unthinkable."

"Well, Brother Ezra went and thought it, Mr. Simpson," Cimarron said, and then he asked one of the roustabouts to bring his black and two of the horses that had been ridden by the Indians in the show's concluding act, all of which were still in the tent the audience had long since vacated.

"Gunther's cats," Simpson said. "Almost any one of us can care for Lucinda's Lipizzaner, but Gunther's lions and leopards—he's the only one who knows how to handle and control them or who dares get close enough to them to feed them. The man loves those beasts and I swear that sometimes I think they love him just as much. Perhaps it has something to do with the way he has always taken such good care of them, the way he . . ."

Cimarron, as the roustabout brought the three horses to him, was no longer listening to what Simpson was saying. Simpson had reminded him of something and that something had given him an idea, an idea that, once transformed into action, would, he began to hope, let him free Brother Ezra's two doomed prisoners. "Point me the way to Gunther's wagon," he said, and when Ramona had done so, he told the roustabout, "Hold these horses for me. I'll be right back."

Once inside Gunther's wagon, he hunted hastily through it and was relieved when he finally located the object of his search. Carrying the bottle he had taken from a trunk, he made his way back to where the circus people still stood talking among themselves in worried tones. "Anybody happen to have a bottle of whiskey they'd let me have?"

"I have one," Babe answered. "I'll get it."

When she returned with a nearly full bottle of whiskey, Cimarron placed it in his saddlebag along with the smaller bottle he had taken from Gunther's wagon. Then, after looping lengths of rope around the necks of the two circus horses, he swung into the saddle of his horse and, leading the other two mounts, rode away from the lot with Davey's cry of "Good luck!" and Babe's "Godspeed" echoing in his ears.

He rode to the north, Paradise on his right, and when he reached the eastern edge of the town, he dismounted and tied the two horses to a cottonwood. He took Babe's bottle of whiskey from his saddlebag and opened it. Then he removed the bottle he had taken from Gunther's wagon. After opening it, he poured nearly half of its contents into the whiskey. He returned the smaller bottle to his saddlebag, boarded his horse, and singing in a low slurred voice and waving the whiskey bottle merrily in the air, rode into Paradise.

No lights were visible in the windows of the homes and stores he passed. The moon was down and the stars shed little light as, following Ramona's directions, he made his way to the building that housed the office of Paradise's justice of the peace.

"Oh, bury me out on the lone prairie," he sang from the song called "The Dying Cowboy." "The words came low and mournfully." He hiccupped as loud as he could, got out of the saddle, and began to pound on the door of the building that had been his destination. ". . . From the cold, pale lips of a youth who lay on his dying couch at the close of day." He pounded harder on the door, but stopped when he felt the muzzle of a rifle ram into the small of his back. He hiccupped again, louder than the first time.

"Don't move," said a male voice from behind him.

"I'm hardly even able to," Cimarron said cheerfully. He raised the bottle and the whiskey inside it sloshed about.

"This stuff's on the verge of turning me to stone, which is why I'm here."

"Why are you here?" the same male voice asked suspiciously.

"I'm looking for a bunk to bed down on till I sober up. Figured the jail would be a place to find one if you folks in town happen to be hospitable."

"We are. We're also God-fearing. But we've got no jail you can sleep in."

"No jail?" Cimarron's thoughts raced. "I've got no money to rent a room in your hotel, so I guess I'll just have to move on. If you'll be kind enough to let me, that is."

"Fork your horse, stranger."

"I'll do that, yes, sir, I'll do that very thing right now and I do thank you for not drilling me." As the rifle barrel was withdrawn from his back, Cimarron turned and, lowering his voice, whispered, "Have a drink on me. This here whiskey's near to ninety proof and it's strong enough to make a man happy even before it hits his gut." He held out the bottle to the man, who took a step away from him. "Go on, have a swig."

"Can't. I've got prisoners round back I got to guard."

"Well, I'm not a man to make another commit dereliction of duty, but one swig doesn't even come close to being a crime." Cimarron paused, grinned. "You're afraid of being seen, is that it? Well, then, come on around back where you'll be out of sight." Without waiting for a response, Cimarron, staggering and waving the whiskey bottle, started around the side of the building. When he heard footsteps behind him, he turned and, swaying giddily, put a finger to his lips and whispered, *"Sshhhh!"*

Once behind the building, he offered the bottle to the man with the rifle.

The man took it and then called out softly, "Trent. Sullivan."

A man appeared from a grove of aspens in the distance, a rifle cradled in his arm. Another man appeared out of the darkness shed by the building's eaves. He dropped down to the ground from the overhang above the back entrance to the building and, carrying his rifle, came up to stand facing Cimarron.

"What's up, Harley?" he asked of the man holding the whiskey bottle.

"This drifter showed up out front a minute or two ago. Brought this." He held up the bottle and smiled.

As Harley put down his rifle and took a drink, Cimarron looked around and spotted the two dark shapes on the ground not far away. "What's them?" he asked innocently as Trent and then Sullivan, who had joined them, drank, although he knew what they were.

"Our prisoners," Sullivan answered. "We caught us a witch and a warlock tonight and we staked them out under those buffalo hides to keep till we can burn 'em alive come dawn."

Cimarron moved away from the makeshift prisons, his eyes widening. "A witch, you say? I steer clear of such women as are witches." You're a damned liar, he thought, before asking, "What's a warlock?"

"A he-witch," Trent told him.

Cimarron moved still farther away and watched Harley take a second drink from the bottle before offering it to Trent, who leaned his rifle against a tree and took it in one hairy hand.

"That's sure powerful stuff," Harley observed, wiping his lips with the back of his hand. "I feel woozy already after only two swallows."

"Told you it packed a punch," Cimarron reminded him, and watched Sullivan put down his rifle and take a long drink from the bottle.

"Here," Sullivan said, and handed Cimarron the bottle.

"Much obliged." Cimarron put the bottle to his lips, tilted it, and pretended to take a drink. He passed the bottle to Harley, who took it and drank deeply from it.

The bottle made one more round.

Harley was the first to fall. He lay limply on the ground, moaning softly.

"The man, it seems, can't hold his liquor," Cimarron observed, sadly shaking his head and then grinning as Trent's body buckled and the guard collapsed on the ground, to be followed only moments later by Sullivan.

He ran to the nearer of the two buffalo hides and began to boot loose the pegs that held it on the ground. Moments later, he was helping Gunther to his feet.

"I thought it was your voice I heard," Gunther said, stretching and staring down at the three comatose guards.

Cimarron said nothing as he kicked loose several pegs pinning the other buffalo hide to the ground. He raised the hide and helped Lucinda crawl out from under it.

"Cimarron," she cried, and threw herself into his arms. "I was so frightened—so terrified! Oh, I'm glad you're here."

"Honey, I'm so glad you're *here*," he said, hugging her, keenly conscious of her lush breasts pressed against his chest and of Gunther's scowl. "But now all of us've got to get the hell out of Paradise. Gunther, you take one of those guards and I'll take another one and let's *go!*"

Once out in front of the building, Cimarron threw Trent's body over the neck of his horse and then swung into the saddle. He helped Lucinda up behind him and then, with Gunther loping beside the dun, Harley's body slung over his shoulder, he rode east out of the town toward the spot where he had tied the two horses.

Once there, Lucinda and Gunther mounted the two horses he had brought for them, and following him, they galloped along the northern border of Paradise, heading west.

As they continued riding hard, Harley's body, which Gunther had draped over his mount's neck, bounced until Gunther put one big hand on it to steady it.

When they reached the circus lot, they drew rein and dismounted.

"What do we do with these two?" Gunther asked Cimarron, indicating the unconscious forms of Trent and Harley.

"You got someplace we can put them where they won't cause us any trouble?" Cimarron asked, and Gunther promptly pointed to a wagon in which a lion paced back and forth, its golden eyes glowing in the light of the torches dotting the lot.

"That lion's likely to cause Harley and Trent some trouble if you put them in there with him."

Gunther shook his head. "I will put in a partition to make a safety cage for them. Caesar will be in one half of the wagon and these two in the other half."

"Won't they be surprised when they wake up face to face with Caesar," Lucinda said, and smiled. Gunther also smiled, and picked up Trent and Harley and carried them toward the cage wagon.

Someone shouted out the news that Gunther and Lucinda were back, and she and Cimarron were soon surrounded by a crowd demanding to know what had happened and how he had managed to rescue Brother Ezra's prisoners.

"I remembered," he said, "hearing Gunther say that he had to buy some tincture of nicotine to put one of his leopards to sleep so he could treat its hurt paw. I poured some of that stuff into the bottle of whiskey I got from Babe and gave the boys a few drinks, which put them to sleep almost as fast as a sober man can spit. It was the only thing I could think of to do. Guns wouldn't have done no good and maybe a whole lot of bad."

Simpson came scurrying through the crowd. He embraced Lucinda and then Gunther. "Well done, Cimarron," he boomed. "Very well done indeed!"

"We'd best be moving out of here," Cimarron advised. "It strikes me that Brother Ezra and his boys'll be mad as hornets get at a bear who's robbing their hive when he finds out that his witch and warlock have flown the coop. How fast can you folks move out?"

The crowd exploded in all directions as if in answer to Cimarron's question and the world of the circus began to disappear as wagons were quickly loaded and tents were swiftly brought down to the ground.

The noise that had so suddenly erupted in the night caused first Harley and then Trent to stir and then to awaken.

Both men screamed simultaneously as Caesar let out an ear-shattering roar and thrust a huge paw between the bars of the partition separating him from them.

They scrambled back to the far end of the safety cage, their faces white, their eyes wide with terror.

Lucinda linked her arm in Cimarron's. "Will you walk me to my wagon?" she inquired.

"Glad to."

As they walked across the lot, Lucinda tightened her grip on Cimarron's arm and said, "I'm glad you don't think I'm a witch as did that misguided zealot Brother Ezra."

"Witches are said to be old and ugly and evil. But you're young and as pretty as new paint on a barn."

"I can be evil, though."

"You can?"

"Well, what I really mean is I can be evil by the silly standards of very narrow-minded people."

"Witch-evil? You mean you can cast spells on people? Make them do bad things?"

Lucinda cocked her head to one side and gave Cimarron a sly glance. "You might put it that way. I have been considering quite seriously casting a spell on you, Cimarron."

"One that would make me do something bad—bad by the silly standards of those narrow-minded people you mentioned?" When Lucinda smiled instead of answering his question, Cimarron grinned and said, "I don't need no witch-woman to cast a spell on me to make me do those kinds of things. My pa, he was a righteous man, and he once told me in a fit of pique over my shenanigans with the local girls I went to school with as a boy that he could almost swear I'd been *born* knowing how to do those sorts of things."

"I'm delighted to hear that because, to be perfectly honest, I really don't know how to cast a spell on you, Cimarron."

"Sure, you do. You just keep looking at me the way you have been and staying so close to me like you're doing at the moment, and that's enough to put me under your spell. Question is, what are we going to do about this spell you've gone and put me under?''

"Here's my wagon. Come inside and we'll talk about it.''

As Cimarron followed Lucinda into her wagon, he said, "It wasn't so much talking I had in mind as it was—''

She placed a finger on his lips to silence him and then lit a lamp and closed and latched the door.

Cimarron looked around. At the tiny table covered with a fringed purple shawl. At the neatly made bunk against one wall, on which rested a floppy cotton doll with round black eyes that seemed to be staring at him. At the photograph of Lucinda and her Lipizzaner on the wall. He went over and stood in front of it, his hands thrust into the back pockets of his jeans.

Lucinda came up behind him and removed his hat, which she placed on a chair that sat near the door. "I sell copies of those photographs to the townies between the menagerie display and the circus performance after I autograph them. I have them made up by the gross.'' She put her hands on Cimarron's shoulders and turned him toward her.

His hands came out of his pockets and he drew her close to him. Then he bent and kissed her, pressing his pelvis against her as he did so.

Their lips parted and Lucinda began to unbutton his shirt. After she had slipped it off, Cimarron unbuckled his gun rig and let it drop to the floor.

"You were marvelous,'' Lucinda sighed as she hurriedly began to undress.

Cimarron, sitting on the edge of the bunk and pulling off his boots, said, "That's what I'd hoped you'd say after we finished up. It seems a strange thing to tell a man beforehand.''

"You don't understand. I was referring to your battle with Crocker.'' Lucinda, naked, lay down on the bed.

Cimarron skinned out of his jeans and lay down beside her, aware of the heat of her body and aware too of his hunger for

116

her, which was rising within him at the same time his shaft was swiftly rising to probe her thigh.

Suddenly, she rolled over on top of him. With her hands pressing down upon his shoulders and her pelvis rubbing against his, she looked down at him. "Tell me what it felt like."

Cimarron caught the odd light in her eyes and remembered having seen it before—when she had spoken to him after he had killed Crocker. "Tell you what what felt like?"

"How you felt when you killed Crocker." She reached down, gripped him, and eased him into her, settling on him and then beginning to twist her hips slightly. "I'll bet it felt good."

"It felt bad. I take no pleasure in killing."

Lucinda's body stiffened. She stopped moving. "No," she whispered. "Don't say that. Tell me it was good. Tell me how you felt when you put the knife into him the way I just put you inside me."

"Honey, it wasn't—it was—I—"

"Do it!" Lucinda screamed at him. "Tell me what it felt like. If you don't, I won't be able to— You want me to enjoy this, don't you? You don't care just about yourself, do you?"

Cimarron wearily turned his head to one side, trying to concentrate on the slick warmth and wetness surrounding his shaft, wanting to explode and then withdraw and dress and go away to a place where there was no woman like Lucinda, who could be aroused only by lurid descriptions of how it felt to kill a man.

"Please, Cimarron," she pleaded. When he mutely shook his head, she groaned, her face contorted. But then, as her hips began to swivel again, she brightened. "If you won't tell me, I'll tell you." She drew a deep eager breath. "You have the knife in your hand. Crocker's coming at you. He's going to kill you. You stab him and the knife—you can feel it cut into his body, the very center of his being. You feel his blood on your hand and you smile and then you twist the knife. First one way. Then the other. You rip . . ."

Lucinda threw back her head, her neck arched, and cried out wordlessly, her nails biting into Cimarron's shoulders. "The sharp knife—the blood . . ." Her body began to throb.

Cimarron, as she rose and fell upon him, shaking with ecstasy, felt himself flood her, causing her to cry out a second time and throw herself down upon him.

"You must have killed other men besides Crocker," she murmured a moment later, her words muffled because her face was buried in the pillow. "How, Cimarron? With your gun? Your hands?" She groped about until she found his unbandaged hand. She raised her head and kissed it. "What was it like? It was good, wasn't it?"

Cimarron, swiftly softening, slid out of her.

She reached down and began to stroke him. "In a minute," she said softly, "I'll have it hard again."

Several minutes passed during which he failed to respond to the touch of her hands or her tongue on his softened flesh.

"Some other time, Lucinda," he told her, knowing full well that there would be no other time for them because he felt, in some strange and altogether unpleasant way, that he had been defiled by her. He wondered how an act of such intimacy, which should have brought them close together in a more than merely physical way, had made him feel as if an impenetrable wall had suddenly risen between them. He slid out from under her, got up, and began to dress.

She lay silently on the bed watching him, seeming to devour him with her eyes, which roamed over his torso, lingered lasciviously on his genitals, glided down along the length of his strong legs.

"Come back soon," she whispered, her voice light and lilting.

Cimarron continued dressing, saying nothing as he fought to forget the awful light that he had been shining in her eyes when she had spoken so sensuously of his knife and Crocker's blood.

"Next time," she murmured, "you must tell me about the other men you've killed. I'm sure there must have been

118

others. There were others, weren't there? How many others, Cimarron?''

"I don't notch my gun nor keep count," he answered, and left the wagon without another word.

He moved through the night toward his own wagon as other wagons moved slowly west past him, trying not to think of what had just happened, trying hard to forget that it had happened in such an ugly way.

When he reached his wagon, he changed places with Davey, ordering him to get some sleep.

"I'm glad you didn't get hurt back there in Paradise," Davey said before climbing down from the wagon seat.

Cimarron thought of Crocker, who had been hurt for the last time in his life. And then of Lucinda, whose lust was inextricably bound up with such fatal hurting. He drove on, shaking his head, his thoughts as black as the night around him.

The sun was rising above the eastern horizon as the circus train emerged from the Sandstone Hills and moved out across the Red Bed Plains where prickly-stemmed buffalo bur grew, the weed's tiny yellow flowers glowing in the day's first light.

The sky above Cimarron was a pale cloudless blue and he yawned as he let his team plod on at their own steady pace. He yawned a second time and then, dropping the reins, stood up and stretched.

He quickly sat down as the crack of a rifle shot sullied the pure morning air, and he looked around the side of the wagon. He was not surprised to see the riders coming out of the Sandstone Hills toward the circus train, guns in their hands as they spurred their mounts. He pounded the fist of his uninjured hand on the wagon and yelled, "Davey!"

When Davey had climbed up beside him, he said, "Take the reins. Hold the team. Don't let the horses bolt. You can do that?''

Davey nodded and Cimarron climbed down to the ground

and went running toward the lead wagon. "Take cover," he shouted to the startled circus people as he ran. "Brother Ezra and some of his boys are coming after us. Take cover inside the wagons."

As men and women, some with fear on their faces, obeyed his command, he ran on until he reached the cage wagon that held the lion Caesar as well as Harley and Trent.

Caesar snarled.

Harley yelled, "Now Brother Ezra's going to make you pay for what you did to us."

"And pay a pretty steep price at that," Trent gloated gleefully.

Cimarron stood beside the cage, and as Brother Ezra and his men reached the circus train and divided their forces on each side of it, he took off his stetson and waved it in the air. "Hey, you Bible-thumping bastard, you," he yelled. "You it is I'm talking to, Brother Ezra!"

Brother Ezra, his mount wheeling beneath him, stared hard at Cimarron and said, "We have come to administer justice to all of you, not just to the witch and the warlock, because someone among you dared to free my prisoners last night."

"You're looking right smack at that someone," Cimarron shouted.

Brother Ezra gave a signal and the man next to him shouldered his carbine, pointing it at Cimarron.

"You shoot," Cimarron shouted down to the man, "and your boys'll be breakfast for this lion, who's not at all inclined to be what you could call neighborly."

Brother Ezra's eyes narrowed as he noticed Harley and Trent for the first time.

"Shoot him," Trent cried. "And then let us out of here."

Brother Ezra's eyes flicked to the man with the carbine at his side.

"See this here?" Cimarron called out. He gripped the movable partition that separated Caesar from the two men in the safety cage. "All I got to do is pull this out and your boys are goners."

He ducked as a shot from the carbine *pinged* over his head and then he partially removed the partition.

As Caesar, bellying down on the floor of his cage, tried to thrust a paw around the partition, Cimarron's eyes remained riveted on Brother Ezra's face.

"Maybe you can kill me," he yelled to Brother Ezra, "and a whole lot of the rest of us too, but you got to be willing to give up on Harley and Trent if that's the move you decide to make. Is it? Or haven't you got the stomach for that?"

"Brother Ezra," a man called out from the opposite side of the circus train. "It's me—Ted Trent. You wouldn't let him do that to my brother, would you?"

Cimarron saw the lust for killing flare in Brother Ezra's eyes and it reminded him of what he had seen flare similarly in Lucinda's eyes earlier. He waited, his hands gripping the partition, ready to remove it.

"No!" Trent screamed from inside the safety cage, gripping the outer bars with both hands, his back to Caesar. "Oh, *noooo*!"

"You do like I tell you," Cimarron shouted to Brother Ezra, "or I'll feed your two boys to Caesar." Without waiting for a response, he continued, "Throw your guns in the creek over there, every man jack of you!"

Slowly and with evident reluctance, Brother Ezra and his men began to dismount and do as they had been ordered to do.

When the last gun was beneath the surface of Mustang Creek, Cimarron yelled, "Davey!"

When Davey came racing up to the cage wagon, Cimarron ordered him to drive off the horses belonging to Brother Ezra and his men.

As Davey slapped the rump of the horse nearest to him and it went racing away to the south with its stirrups flapping wildly, Brother Ezra cried, "No!"

Cimarron, when he saw Davey hesitate, shouted, "Yes!" At the same instant, he eased the partition out enough for Caesar to thrust his front paw past it.

The lion roared and tried to seize its terrified prey just beyond the protective bars.

Davey ran off a second horse and then a third. A fourth.

When all the horses had gone galloping away, Cimarron slid the partition back into place, forcing Caesar to withdraw his paw. He straightened and unholstered his revolver. "Now then, boys, you can all start walking back to Paradise."

"Walk back?" Brother Ezra bellowed.

"What about Harley and Trent?" one of the men asked.

"I'll let them loose," Cimarron answered, "once I've seen the last of you drop down over the eastern horizon. Now, get a move on!"

Later, when Brother Ezra and his men were nothing more than a small black blur against the rising sun, Cimarron holstered his Colt.

"You said you were going to let those men go," Davey remarked, pointing at Harley and Trent.

"Oh, I'll let them loose. When the time's right. At the moment, though, we'll be better off if they stay right where they are. With them keeping Caesar company, Brother Ezra and his boys aren't likely to come calling on us a second time."

Caesar growled and then roared, giving Cimarron a yellow-eyed glance that he thought looked decidedly disappointed, not to mention reproachful.

8

In the afternoon, after fording the Washita River, Cimarron ordered the circus train to halt and make camp.

As fires were built and the stock was watered at the river's edge, he went in search of Gunther, and when he found the man, he asked him for the key to Caesar's wagon, which Gunther promptly gave him.

"You are going to free those two men now?"

"I am. I don't reckon we can expect any more trouble from them or their friends." Cimarron left Gunther and made his way to the cage wagon.

When Trent and Harley saw him coming, both men began to plead with him to release them.

"I'm about to do that very thing," Cimarron announced. But as he was about to insert the key Gunther had given him in the padlock on the cage's door, he heard the sound of a distant shot. "Damn it all to hell," he muttered, and turned to the east, where the shot had been fired. "If that's Brother Ezra and his boys back again," he told his prisoners, "I'm going to feed both them and you to Caesar this time." He drew his revolver and peered into the distance.

One rider, he thought, and he's riding hell-bent-for-election in this direction. Was he the one who fired that shot or was he the one who got himself fired at? he asked himself.

He pulled his stetson down low on his forehead to block the sun from his eyes and squinted into the distance at the second rider he had just spotted some distance behind the first. Lawman, he thought as the sun glinted on the nickel badge the man wore on his shirt.

As the second rider, using his reins to lash his horse, came closer, Cimarron recognized the man. Henderson, he thought. That's Deputy Len Henderson. He ran to where his black was tied behind his wagon, freed the horse, and swung into the saddle.

"Where are you going?" Gunther called out to him as Cimarron turned the horse and rode, without bothering to answer the question, out of the camp, heading straight for the man Henderson was pursuing.

As he rode into the Washita, Henderson's quarry entered it on the eastern side. The man turned and fired at Henderson. He missed. He fired a second time and this time Cimarron, as his horse swam toward Henderson's attacker, saw Henderson, who had been hit, lose his grip on his mount's reins and slide from the saddle and into the river.

Cimarron fired a warning shot over the head of the man who had shot Henderson, but the rider neither slowed his horse nor turned it. Instead, he fired at Cimarron and his bullet grazed the side of the black, causing the horse to scream and begin to founder.

When the man reached a position opposite Cimarron, he took aim again, but before he could fire, Cimarron slid down along the side of his horse and then under the surface of the water, losing his stetson in his desperate maneuver to avoid being shot. He clung tightly to his saddle horn with his free hand while holding his Colt above the surface of the water with his right. Holding his breath, he remained underwater for what seemed to him an interminable time. Soon his lungs—every single cell in his body—seemed to him to be screaming their demand for air, but he remained submerged until he felt himself growing dizzy. Only then did he haul himself back into the saddle and begin to battle for control of the wounded and terrified horse beneath him. He managed to turn the horse after a brief struggle with it, and gulping great drafts of air, he spurred it savagely and sent it swimming back to the west bank of the Washita.

Minutes later, as the man Henderson had been pursuing came out of the river, he turned to confront the oncoming Cimarron, his six-gun raised.

Cimarron, still thigh-deep in water, fired two swift shots.

He swore when he saw that, because the unstable black beneath him had lurched as he fired, both shots had missed the mounted man on the riverbank.

One more try, he told himself, and again brought the hammer of his gun to full cock.

The black reared and screamed as Cimarron's spur accidentally struck the bloody gash on the horse's flank where the bullet had grazed the animal.

He was thrown from the saddle and his head hit the ground hard. The force of his fall knocked the gun from his hand. He caught a hazy glimpse of the grin on the face of the man who had shot at him, saw his horse shake the water from its body and then stand trembling on the riverbank, heard someone—a woman he couldn't see—cry out as the gun in the mounted man's hand lowered and the gunman sighted along its barrel . . .

He tried to roll to the side, willing his numb body to obey the command his mind was giving it, when he heard the man let out a loud yell and he saw a long leather whip suddenly whirl through the air, coil around the gunman's right wrist, and then grow abruptly taut.

As Cimarron struggled to his knees, the haze surrounding him gradually thinning, he saw the gun fall from his attacker's hand, saw Babe, tottering on the thick pillars of her legs, run forward and throw her bulk down upon it, saw Davey for the first time as he held tightly to the oak handle of the whip while the man he had disarmed struggled to rip it from his wrist.

He got to his feet, retrieved his gun, and standing unsteadily and fighting to keep his body from swaying, said, "Empty your saddle, mister, and empty it real quick!"

As the man reluctantly dismounted, Davey flicked the whip and it fell free of the man's wrist.

"God damn you," the man shouted at Cimarron. "What for did you have to go and get yourself mixed up in this?"

Cimarron threw a quick glance over his shoulder and saw that Henderson was aboard his horse again and swimming it toward the west bank of the river. Just before he looked back at his attacker and Henderson's quarry, he saw Henderson bend down and scoop up the stetson he had lost earlier, which had been floating on the surface of the Washita.

"I hope you'll see fit to tell me what it is I've gone and got myself mixed up in," he said, addressing the gunman, who was grimacing and muttering under his breath.

But he had to wait for Henderson to arrive before he got the information he wanted.

"Cimarron, you old son of a gun, you," Henderson boomed as he rode up and handed Cimarron his hat. "What a sight for tired eyes you are, man, even though you look like a cat somebody put in a sack and tried to drown. What in the name of hell and heaven both are you doing way out here?"

"I've taken up sheepherding, Len," Cimarron told him with a grin. He pointed to the circus people who were standing nearby and watching him. "Those are my sheep. They're heading for California and I'm the one's been assigned to see that they get to the western border of the Territory safe and sound. Now, tell me something, Len. Who the hell's this jasper you were chasing?"

"Bank robber," Henderson replied, his eyes on Babe as several roustabouts helped her get to her feet. "His name's Dave Youngman."

Cimarron stared at Youngman, noting the man's curly blond hair, flabby body, and a protruding stomach that almost buried his belt. He's hardly hip-high to a short horse, he thought.

"He looks familiar to me," Cimarron told Henderson, "but I'll be damned if I can remember where I might have met up with him."

126

"Maybe you didn't," Henderson suggested. "Maybe you seen his picture on a wanted poster somewhere. Lord knows, there's enough of them around the Territory these days."

"Maybe that's why he seems so familiar," Cimarron mused. "He's a bank robber, you say?"

"I'm not," Youngman declared angrily. "I was, once, but I'm not no more. I'm straight, Henderson. Have been for years."

"He robbed the bank back in Fort Smith," Henderson said, unperturbed by Youngman's outburst. "Just before it closed for the day."

"When was that, Len?" When Henderson had told him, Cimarron said, "You put any stock in his claim that he's as innocent as a just-born babe?"

"No, I don't. Witnesses saw him and identified him to Marshal Upham, who, once I got back to Fort Smith, sent me out after him. He robbed the bank in McAlester too. That was two days ago. He's guilty all right. Sure as shit stinks, he is."

Cimarron stared at Youngman, turning over in his mind what Henderson had just told him.

"I didn't rob those banks," Youngman insisted angrily. "You're framing me, Marshal, on account of I did time once in Leavenworth for bank robbery."

"Witnesses I talked to in McAlester," Henderson calmly told Cimarron, "identified him as the man who did the job on their bank. He robbed it late in the afternoon just before it closed up for the day, same as he did with the one in Fort Smith."

"How much did he get away with?"

"Close to five thousand dollars in Fort Smith, some of which happened to be mine, by the way." Henderson scowled at Youngman. "He got over seven thousand in McAlester."

"You got it back from him, though."

"No, I didn't."

"How come?"

"He's gone and hid it away somewheres, but I can guaran-

127

tee you that by the time him and me get back to Fort Smith, I'll have made him tell me where he hid it.'' Henderson, still scowling, raised a clenched fist and shook it at Youngman.

"Those witnesses of yours, Henderson,'' Youngman shouted, "ought to see a doctor about their eyes. You told me yourself the jasper who robbed those banks wore a bandanna that covered half of his face and a derby hat pulled down low on most of the other half.''

"Just like you used to do, Youngman,'' Henderson countered.

"I wore a hat, yes. A *slouch* hat. I wouldn't be caught dead in a derby.''

"Where'd you catch up with him?'' Cimarron asked Henderson. "Was it by any chance back in that hellhole the people who live in it call Paradise?''

Henderson shook his head. "I tracked him west from McAlester. Got close to him just north of Cherokee Town here in Chickasaw Nation. He was heading southwest and we never even got close to Paradise, which was way east of us.''

"Well, you've finally got your hands on him, Len, but he's hurt you in the getting.''

"Not bad, though. Winged me is all he managed to do. He's a better bank robber than he is a sharpshooter.''

"I wish I'd blown you halfway to hell, Henderson,'' Youngman snarled.

"Babe,'' Cimarron said, "do you think maybe you can fix up my deputy marshal friend here?''

"Sure, I can,'' Babe answered, beaming at Henderson and handing him Youngman's gun. "You come right along with me, Deputy, and I'll see to it that you get everything you need—or want.''

"I'm obliged to you, ma'am,'' Henderson said as he stepped down from his saddle. He gave Cimarron a questioning glance.

Cimarron raised his eyebrows and shrugged noncommittally.

Then, as Henderson, leading his horse, walked away with Babe, Cimarron beckoned to Davey, who followed him as he marched Youngman over to the cage wagon where Caesar prowled restlessly, his yellow eyes alight.

He unlocked the padlock and let Harley and Trent go racing away to the east. Then, gesturing with his gun, he ordered Youngman to enter the safety cage, which the man did with evident reluctance. After relocking the cage door, he turned and, indicating the whip in Davey's hand, asked, "Where'd you get that thing?"

"It belongs to Mr. Kleist," Davey answered. "When I saw what was happening—I've got no gun, not even a knife—I wanted to help you out if I could, only I didn't know how or what to do, but then I remembered this''—Davey held up the whip—"and I went and found it in Mr. Kleist's wagon, and then— Well, you know the rest."

"You used that whip better'n most men use a gun. I'm grateful to you for what you did."

"Before Pa took to drinking so bad, he was a freighter. I grew up learning how to handle one of these things on the mules Pa drove. He taught me to use it."

"He taught you well and you learned your lesson as well, looks to me like. I'd have been carrying lead around in me if you hadn't been so quick with that whip. Or maybe I might be dead. I'll tell you something, boy, and I'll tell it to you true. You're welcome at my fire anytime."

"That's sure good to hear, Cimarron. But all I did was what I suppose any assistant deputy United States marshal would have done, considering what was going on." Davey grinned.

So did Cimarron. "Boy, there's some things I want you to do for me if you're willing."

"I'm willing, Cimarron. What things?"

"First off, see to my horse. He's been hit by one of Youngman's bullets, but not bad. Miss Folsom's likely to have the first-aid box in her wagon along with Deputy Henderson. See if you can borrow it from her when she's through with it." Cimarron told Davey how he wanted the horse treated and then, "I'm going to get out of these wet

129

clothes and dry them out, and while I'm doing that and after you're through with my mount, I want you to take a little ride on him—into Paradise. Keep your head low and your eyes on the prowl and try not to let anybody recognize you. Now, here's what I want you to do for me once you get to town."

When Cimarron had finished telling Davey what he wanted done, Davey went to the black and led it in the direction of Babe's wagon.

Cimarron turned and went to his wagon. Once inside it, he stripped, wrapped a blanket about his loins, and then went outside and hung his clothes up to dry.

He was asleep on his bunk when he was awakened by a knock on the door of his wagon. "Come on in," he called out, and then yawned and stretched as Henderson climbed into the wagon. "Babe got you all fixed up, did she, Len?"

"Cimarron, you're not going to believe this, but it really happened. Just now, it did." Henderson sat down on a chair and, as Cimarron, naked, sat up on the edge of his bed, continued, "That boxcar of a woman offered me ten dollars if I'd drop my pants and slip it to her."

"Ten dollars," Cimarron repeated in a neutral tone.

"I could have used the ten dollars too. I could have used the *twenty* dollars she offered me when I told her I liked my ladies on the lean side. But that didn't discourage her, not one whit did it. She upped the ante to twenty-five dollars, damned if she didn't."

"Babe must have been taken by your good looks, Len, and your fancy manners."

"Don't kid me, Cimarron. I look more like a fox than some foxes do. And I've got the manners of a mountebank. That big tub of lard's just so hard-up she'd even proposition *me*."

"I never before knew you to turn down the chance to roll in the hay with a willing lady, Len."

"Oh, Babe was willing all right, but what the hell, Cimarron! I mean, I'd've probably never been able to find her hole that she wanted me to plug so bad. She must weigh half a ton at least, maybe more.''

"What's her weight got to do with it, Len? I mean, she could've given you a damned good run for your—I mean, for her—money. When the wanting's on a woman—any woman—a man's, it seems to me, either a fool or a sissy not to take what she's as anxious as a squirrel storing nuts for winter to give him. And in Babe's case, to pay him for taking it, to boot.''

"Well, I'm no sissy, Cimarron, as you damned well know, and I don't think I'm a fool—not most of the time, I'm not, anyway. But think on it. What if she rolled over on me while we were going at it hot and heavy? What if she did? I'd've been pressed flatter'n a flapjack.''

As Henderson erupted in rowdy laughter, Cimarron got up, wrapped his blanket around himself, and went to the open door of the wagon. He looked up at the sun in the sky. Late afternoon, he thought, and still hot as Hades. He climbed down the steps and felt his clothes. His jeans, shirt, and socks were dry, but his stetson was still damp.

Henderson came out of the wagon as he was gathering up his clothes and said, "I'll be moseying on back to Fort Smith now, Cimarron. What'd you do with Youngman?''

Cimarron pointed.

Henderson gasped until he noticed the partition that separated Youngman from Caesar.

"Here's the key to the cage," Cimarron said, and handed it to Henderson. "Bring it back to me before you leave. And good luck with your bank robber.''

A memory flared unsummoned in Cimarron's mind—a memory of Ernie Wilcox, who had also protested his innocence of the charge of murder just as Youngman had done on the lesser charge of bank robbery.

He was almost fully dressed when Henderson returned the key to Caesar's cage to him and then departed.

Youngman, his hands handcuffed behind his back, walked,

his head down and his shoulders slumping, in front of Henderson's horse.

Cimarron left his wagon and went to where the circus cook had built a fire and was busily frying ham and eggs. Before he reached the fire, he halted, listening. Someone was quietly weeping somewhere. Where? He looked around. There was no one near him. But the sound continued and he finally realized it was coming from Babe's wagon. He went up to its door, knocked on it, waited. The weeping stopped. The door remained closed. He knocked again.

When Babe finally opened the door, she glared at him. "What do you want?"

"I was on my way to eat something. Thought you might want to keep me company."

Babe's red eyes peered at him suspiciously. "I'm not hungry." She slammed the wagon's door.

Cimarron hesitated a moment and then made his way to the cook's fire. "I'll have two plates of ham and eggs and some of those biscuits," he told the harried man who was juggling Dutch ovens and two thirty-inch frypans in which dozens of eggs were sizzling. "One for me and one for Babe Folsom. I'll help myself since you've got your hands full, looks like." He did, and then carried the two plates he had filled back to Babe's wagon. He slammed a boot against its door and called out, "Babe!"

When her door remained closed, he yelled, "Open up, Babe, or these vittles'll get as cold as a sidewinder's heart."

The door opened a crack. "I told you. I'm not hungry."

"Well, dammit, woman, I am. Now, let me in before I die of starvation aggravated by a bad case of being lonesome."

The door eased open and Cimarron climbed into the wagon. He put the plates down on a table and pulled out a chair, one that had been, he noted, especially built and solidly reinforced for Babe.

She subsided into it and he sat down next to her.

"Here—I brought eating irons." He handed her a knife and fork and began to use his own in an attack on his plate,

132

which was heaped high with food. "Good," he said, the word mangled because his mouth was full. "Try some." He pointed with his knife at Babe's plate.

When she began to eat with no enthusiasm, he said, "You fixed my friend up fine and I thank you for that."

Babe sniffed.

"Len appreciated what you did for him. He told me so." Cimarron continued to devour the food on his plate. "Like I told you before, Babe, you have a tender way of treating a man who's hurting."

Babe's fork fell to the floor as she burst into tears.

"Hey, now, honey, what's wrong?" Cimarron put down his knife and fork and reached out to Babe. His arm went only halfway around her huge body.

"You know. I bet he told you, damn him!"

"Len? He didn't tell me anything worth listening to. What is it I'm supposed to know?"

"I offered him money," Babe sobbed, her tears two tiny creeks streaming down the mountains of her cheeks. "It's not the first time I offered to pay a man to—to— Some of the townies, they take my money—and me. But your friend, he just laughed at me. Oh, I've had men laugh at me before for the same damned reason. I just never do learn, though. I keep hoping. Sometimes I even *pray* that someone will want me— that there'll be a man in a town somewhere who won't look at me and see only that I'm so fat."

Her voice changed, softened. "He'll be tall and slender, the man I'm talking about. His eyes—they'll be dark. Black. Maybe brown. His hair will be curly and his cheeks and chin clean-shaven. He'll come to the grind show—the sideshow— and he'll see me and later he'll wait for me and he'll ask me to go into town with him and I'll say I will and we'll go to a restaurant and he'll never notice how people stare at me and snicker . . ."

Babe pushed her plate away. She folded her arms on the table and laid her head down upon them. Her body shook as she sobbed heartbrokenly.

"Babe."

Her sobs became louder.

"Babe, listen to me. Look at me. *I'm* tall and slender. But then maybe you don't take kindly to green-eyed men."

Babe slowly raised her head and looked at Cimarron. She wiped the tears from her eyes with fisted hands. She opened her mouth and then closed it again.

"I know I'm not much of a prize for a lady like you, Babe. But I'd be glad to take you to town—the very next one we come to—and the two of us could go to a restaurant together and have ourselves a real fine meal, even a bottle of champagne if the town turns out to have one for sale somewhere. Then, later on, we could either come back here to your wagon or stay in a hotel in the town I'm talking about and, well, sort of let things take their natural course the real nice way they tend to do when a man like me has a hankering for a fine woman such as yourself."

"You—" Babe stared at Cimarron. "Why would you—"

"Want you, Babe?"

She nodded, her blue eyes glistening.

"Well, there's a couple or three reasons why. On account of I like you a lot is the first of them. On account of you were good to me when I got knifed back along the trail is the second." Cimarron held up his hand that was covered with its still-damp bandage. "And on account of I'm a hopelessly horny bastard who can't resist a wonderful woman like yourself who has such smooth skin"—he reached out and touched her cheek gently—"and golden hair as fine as spun silk and a body born to comfort the kind of man I just admitted I am."

"Oh, Cimarron!" Babe seized him and crushed his body against hers. "I feel like such a fool for the way I lied to you the day we first met back in Fort Smith—the way I tried to make you believe that I had had so many men. The truth is—"

"To hell with the truth, Babe. Lies are sometimes better than the truth. Especially some of the ones people like to tell themselves when they're feeling lonely and kind of lost the way I sometimes do. You know what I tell myself, come those times?''

Babe released him and shook her head.

''I tell myself I'm not in the slightest scar-faced. I tell myself that the woods are chock full of women who are just waiting to come running to me the minute I crook my finger at them. I tell myself I'm going to live, like they say in storybooks, 'happily ever after.' Lies, Babe, every last one of them, but they do soothe a man when his boot heels are worn way down and his heart's as heavy as the horse he happens to be riding.''

''Oh, Cimarron, do you feel that way too sometimes? Like you haven't got a friend left in the world or the slightest hope for a happier day?''

''Sure, I do. But then I meet a lady like you and I cheer up real quick and go right after her with my hat thrown back and my spurs a-jingling.'' Cimarron leaned over and kissed Babe's full lips.

Her arms went around him as his hands came to rest on her hips.

When their kiss ended, she said, ''Are you sure you really want to—''

He answered her without words. He pulled down the bodice of her dress. His hands went around one of her breasts. His head bent and his lips touched its nipple. His tongue slid from between his lips and caressed it.

''Oh,'' she sighed. And then she was pushing him away and rising. She quickly undressed and then shyly looked down at the floor, her hands flexing nervously, as if they were seeking something to do.

''You are one whole helluva lot of woman, Babe.'' Cimarron hurriedly got out of his clothes, and after Babe had lain down on her bed, he lay down beside her.

Her hands soon found something to do, delighting him. So did her lips, causing him to snap erect.

As he maneuvered himself so that he was finally on top of her and then deep within her, he sighed and said, ''I sure was right before when I told you you had a body that was born to comfort the kind of man I am. Babe, the way you have of taking me to you makes me feel the world's one fine place for me to be living in."

As he began to thrust, his hips rising and falling, Babe's warm arms went around him and her thick legs cuddled against his own.

"Go slow, Cimarron, nice and slow, all right?" she whispered in his ear. "I want it to last."

He obliged. He held himself back, varying his rhythm, and when she gasped and clutched his back, he plunged into her as far as he could go and listened to the sibilant hissing of her breath as she began to shudder and then to moan beneath him.

He remained motionless for a moment and then almost leisurely began to probe again, her body rocking eagerly under him, a great warm ocean of soft and giving flesh. He skillfully caused her to have a second orgasm before allowing himself to increase the speed of his thrusting, which quickly brought him to an explosive and thoroughly satisfying climax.

"Babe," he murmured as he shivered with sensuous pleasure. "Oh, Babe, I do damn myself for a fool for having waited so long to come after you."

"I'm just glad you're here now. If you hadn't come after me pretty soon—well, I think I would have screwed up my courage and come after you. I don't think I could have helped myself. Why, the day you rode onto the lot in Fort Smith and I laid eyes on you for the first time, I almost wet my pants I got so excited."

"Honey, you make a man glad he's alive—and that you are too."

Cimarron withdrew from her and lay by her side, both of them staring up at the roof of the wagon, his left and her right hand clasped together.

"Len Henderson is a fool," he whispered to her several minutes later. "He's downright dim-witted, is what Len Henderson is."

"You mean because he wouldn't—"

"That's exactly what I do mean, honey. But maybe it's best that he turned you down."

"Best?"

"A hot-blooded woman like yourself would have worn him out in no time."

Babe laughed and then, when her laughter had subsided, asked. "Are you worn out?"

"Not nearly."

"Then let's do it again."

They did, and Cimarron, when it finally ended, lay panting beside Babe, contented and relaxed.

Babe turned on her side. "That scar on your face. How did you get it?"

Cimarron told her about the time when he was still a boy helping his father brand calves, and a calf he had roped got away from him, and his father, in a fit of fury, had swung the glowing branding iron he held in his hand. "It raked my face—burned me bad—and left me looking like this," he concluded.

"It seems to me," Babe mused, "that most people—or a lot of them, anyway—have scars of one kind or another. Some you can see. Some you can't."

"Me, I've got both kinds," Cimarron said before he could stop himself, and then, when Babe glanced at him quizzically, he said, "You ought to stop thinking that being fat's the same as being ugly. It's not, Babe."

"But most men—"

"Most men be damned! You'll meet somebody someday, somebody who likes big solid women like yourself who can love a man in ways that lots of skinny women couldn't, no matter how hard they tried."

"We used to have a real skinny man in the grind show. He was billed as The Human Skeleton. He met a woman in one of the towns we played in Missouri and, would you believe it, they got married and he didn't weigh a mite over sixty

137

pounds, soaking wet, on top of which he was missing two of his front teeth.''

"There you go. Don't give up on the game, Babe. You do and it'll turn you as sour as curdled milk. Those big blue eyes of yours'll get a bitter look in them. Those lush lips of yours''—he leaned over and kissed them—"will twist until people will think you're snarling at them, and the fact of the matter is you will be. Give a listen to me, Babe. If a scar-faced and bullet- and knifed-nicked lawman like me can turn the head of a lady from time to time, as I've been lucky enough to do, a pretty blue-eyed golden-haired woman like yourself can do the same thing to a man she's sure to meet one of these days.''

"A dark-eyed man.''

"With curly hair and clean-shaven cheeks and chin.''

Babe threw her great arms around Cimarron and hugged him joyously.

He was hugging her when a knock sounded on the door of the wagon.

"Go away,'' Babe called out sharply, throwing her arms possessively around Cimarron.

"Miss Folsom, it's me—Davey Corliss. I was told that Cimarron's in there with you. Is he?''

"Go away,'' Babe cried.

When Cimarron managed to disentangle himself from her grasp, he kissed her on the tip of her upturned nose and said, "Got to talk to the boy.''

"Don't leave me now, Cimarron.''

"Davey,'' he called out, "you just hold your horses out there. I'll be with you presently.'' He got out of the bed and began to dress.

"I wish you wouldn't go,'' Babe said somewhat forlornly as he pulled on his boots, hopping from one foot to the other as he did so.

"I'll be back. Sometime soon, I hope.''

Davey was waiting for him outside the wagon when he emerged from it.

"What did you find out, boy?"

"The bank in Paradise, it was robbed. I went to a saloon, and while I was eating some of the free lunch there, I heard some men talking about what happened. They said the bank was robbed just before closing time. By a lone man with a sidearm."

Cimarron thoughtfully stroked his chin as he considered the information.

"How did you know the bank in Paradise had been robbed?" Davey asked him.

"Didn't know."

"You guessed?"

Cimarron shook his head.

"A man in the saloon said he was in the bank when it was robbed right around closing time."

"You find out anything else?"

"Sure, I did. I asked questions like you told me to do."

"What kind of answers did you get?"

"The man who was in the bank when it was robbed, he said the robber was a short man. Heavy-set, he said. Then some other man said somebody had told him that the man wasn't heavy-set but fat."

"Did anybody say what kind of gun—or guns—he was toting?"

"One gun. A Navy Colt."

"You find out what the man was wearing, what he looked like?"

"Ordinary clothes, they said. Black pants, brown shirt, high-topped shoes, a derby hat. He had a round face, they said, and he also wore a bandanna."

"Color of his hair? Eyes? Was he bearded? Did he have a mustache?"

"Nobody knew or noticed what color his eyes or hair were. Nobody said he had a beard or a mustache. But neither did they say he didn't have them."

"I'm obliged to you, Davey."

"I'll see to your horse, Cimarron, if you want."

Cimarron walked around to the other side of the black Davey was holding and examined the wound in the animal's flank. "It's starting to pucker already," he commented. "And it looks clean as a whistle. You did a good job on him."

As Davey, smiling happily, led the horse away, Cimarron stood with his hands thrust into the back pockets of his jeans. So the man who had robbed the bank in Paradise was heavyset, he thought. Or fat, depending upon who you talked to. Short. He summoned a mental image of Youngman. That description pretty much fits him, Cimarron decided. He thought back to what Henderson had told him about trailing Youngman. Henderson, he remembered, had said that he had almost caught up with Youngman north of Cherokee Town and then he had trailed him southwest. When I asked him if he'd caught Youngman in Paradise, he said he hadn't. Told me he and Youngman had never even came close to the town, which was off to the east of them.

The nagging suspicion that had been born in his mind earlier as he listened to Henderson and Youngman began to grow.

And, growing right beside it, were two questions.

One: Was it possible that Youngman had been telling the truth when he claimed he hadn't robbed the banks in McAlester and Fort Smith?

Two: Who had robbed the bank in Paradise?

9

In the morning of the fourth day following the freeing of Lucinda and Gunther, the circus train crossed the Chisholm Trail and by afternoon it had reached Traders' Trail.

Cimarron halted the train just west of the trail and told the people he was guiding that they would spend the night camped where they were.

Later, after he had removed Babe's bandage from his hand, which was healing nicely, he joined some of the roustabouts around the communal campfire that had been built, and helped himself to some food. He had just begun to eat when he suddenly put down his plate and got to his feet.

"Something wrong, Cimarron?" one of the men asked him uneasily.

"Don't know for sure. But I just heard something, and since we happen to be on the Kiowa, Comanche, and Apache Reservation . . ." His words trailed away. He stood listening.

A cow bawled in the distance, the sound causing several of the roustabouts to rise to their feet.

"Cattle coming," Cimarron told them. When the first of the longhorns appeared in the south with cowhands riding on both sides of them, Cimarron walked toward the trail boss, who was some distance ahead of the herd.

"You planning on driving straight through the night?" he asked the man when he reached him.

"Considered it," the man replied. "Had some trouble with

Apaches a ways back. Want to get shut of them if I can. But my men are tired and I'm not keen on running my longhorns skinny."

"There's a creek over there," Cimarron told him. "There's good grass all around here. You could do worse in picking a campsite if you're ready to call it quits for today."

The trail boss looked around and then raised an arm and signaled to his two point men. Turning back to Cimarron, he said, "My name's Ed Rhodes."

"Cimarron."

Rhodes dismounted and they shook hands.

"Who are all these people?" Rhodes asked.

Cimarron told him. "They're heading for California, where it's warm and you can pick oranges right in your own backyard, I'm told."

"We're heading for Abilene."

"Where there's nothing, somebody once told me, but the three S's."

"The three S's?"

"Sunshine, sunflowers, and sons of bitches."

Rhodes guffawed. "That somebody told you true, Cimarron. Though there's one or two additional attractions in a rowdy cow town like Abilene."

"I've been there and met those attractions, most of them. You're talking about the red-light ladies, I take it."

"There's not much else in Abilene worth talking about."

As the cowhands bedded the herd down in the distance near the creek, Cimarron asked, "What kind of trouble did the Apaches go and give you, Rhodes?"

"A bunch of them stopped us a few miles back. They wanted us to give them ten beeves they claimed we owed them since the herd was grazing on their grass. I told them I wouldn't give them so much as the sweat off my ass, which didn't set so well with them, I could tell. But the storm blew over pretty quick and they rode on back to wherever it was they came from."

"They were right, though. You are on their land and they

142

can ask for and maybe get payment to let a herd like yours graze on reservation land."

"They'll not get a damned thing from me."

As Rhodes swung into the saddle and then rode away to join his cowhands, Cimarron returned to the fire and sat down by it. When he had finished eating, he took out his pocket knife, opened it, and began to cut away the calluses that covered the palms of his hands.

Occasionally, he looked up at the cattle that were, some of them, standing hock-deep in the creek while others grazed or lay, their legs folded under them, on the ground.

"Cimarron."

He turned his head to find that Gunther had come up behind him. "Have a seat, Gunther."

"I want to say some words to you, Cimarron."

Cimarron stared up into Gunther's cold eyes, noting the tense expression on the man's face. "I'm listening."

"You were told to guide us to the Texas border."

"I'm doing that."

"You were not told to dishonor our women."

Cimarron's eyes narrowed. He rose. "I haven't dishonored any women. What the hell are you talking about, Gunther?"

"Lucinda. She just told me what you and she did. She told me she is in love with you. And I saw Ramona go into your wagon one night not long ago. I am here to tell you to leave Lucinda alone."

"What about Ramona?"

"Stay away from her too."

"Why? Because you want them both for yourself?"

"I want only Lucinda and she will be mine—someday. Soon, I hope. When she learns to believe how much I truly love her."

"You're a damned fool, Gunther," Cimarron said flatly, and saw the fury flare in the animal trainer's eyes. "Lucinda uses you. She makes you chase her but not because she wants to be chased by you. She does it because she wants to hurt Ramona."

143

"I do not understand."

"I know damned well you don't, which is why I called you a fool before. Ramona's in love with you. Lucinda's not and isn't ever likely to be. If you had a lick of sense, you'd leave Lucinda alone and pay attention to Ramona. She's a fine woman."

"You have known her too, then?"

"Nothing happened between Ramona and me. She only came to me because she wanted to make you jealous, to open up your eyes so that you'll maybe be able to see just exactly how much she loves you."

"I love Lucinda."

"Well, I'm sure sorry to hear that, Gunther, on account of you're not her kind of man, not by a long shot, you aren't."

"You are her kind of man? That is what you say to me?"

Cimarron said nothing.

"I am more of a man than you will ever be."

"I'm just not about to debate that point with you, Gunther. All I'm trying to tell you is that Lucinda likes—" How could he explain? he wondered, and then he realized that there was no way for him to do so without the possibility of bringing shame or at least embarrassment to Lucinda. "You ever kill a man, Gunther?"

"No, never."

"That there's what I mean about Lucinda."

"Explain."

"It's not my place to explain. You can ask her about it. She might tell you."

"You must promise me that you will stay away from the women."

"Gunther, you just don't know me very well or you wouldn't go and ask me to promise a thing like that. Why, that's like asking a honey bee to promise to steer clear of roses."

Gunther threw a thick fist in a right cross that cracked against Cimarron's left cheekbone. "I will teach you to be a gentleman. I will make you promise to behave like a decent man."

"You do like that again, Gunther, and I'm going to have to try teaching *you* a lesson or two."

Gunther swung, but Cimarron blunted the blow by turning his body slightly so that Gunther's fist glanced off his shoulder. He delivered a right and then a left jab to the animal trainer's solid body and followed up with a right uppercut that slammed against the man's jaw.

As Gunther staggered backward, Cimarron moved in on him and then ducked as his opponent tried to land a blow on his face. He knocked the man's arm aside and got in one swift punch that struck Gunther's flat stomach, causing the man to grunt.

He waited, and when Gunther had regained his balance and came at him again, he stepped to the side and began to move in a circle, dancing, dodging the blows Gunther attempted to deliver, all of which failed to connect.

"I will kill you if I must," Gunther wheezed, his breath gushing from between his lips.

"You're welcome to try."

Gunther suddenly crouched and came in low, catching Cimarron off guard so that Gunther's hard right fist landed on the left side of his upper body.

"You ought to aim lower," he told Gunther as he sent a fist crashing into the side of the man's head. "You can maybe bust a man's gut if you aim lower."

"Gunther, stop it!" Ramona cried as she stood on the edge of the crowd that had gathered, a mix of circus people and cowhands, to watch the fight. "Cimarron, don't hurt him."

Cimarron caught a glimpse of her and then of Lucinda, who stood not far away, her tongue sliding along her lips, her eyes wide open and eager.

"You heard Ramona, Gunther?" he asked, his fists raised and his boots firmly planted on the ground. "She doesn't want me to hurt you. No woman wants to see the man she loves get hurt. I'm willing to quit if you are."

Gunther lunged at Cimarron, who adroitly sidestepped and

then put out a leg to trip his attacker, sending Gunther sprawling facedown in the dirt.

He bent down, intending to haul the man to his feet, but before he could touch the animal trainer, a cowhand yelled, "Hell's boiling over, boys! Hold the herd!"

The cowhand, who was standing not far from Cimarron, went racing toward the rope corral and the remuda within it.

Another cowhand ran after him and then all the cowhands were racing away from the scene of the fight. Cimarron, straightening, saw the cattle, almost all of them on their feet now, milling about uncertainly and bawling nervously.

He was only vaguely aware of Ramona running past him toward the downed Gunther. He had spotted the cause of the herd's restlessness and was about to let out a yell to alert the cowhands to it when he was spun around and Gunther's fist smashed into his face, opening a cut on his right cheek, which began to bleed freely.

"Stampede!" Rhodes yelled at the top of his voice, running on foot toward the steers that were leading it, waving his arms wildly in a vain effort to stop the headlong rush.

Cimarron, as sweat leaked into his eyes, blinked and swung on the blurred figure of Gunther in front of him. His left fist glanced off the man's right shoulder and his right caught Gunther below the jaw, snapping the animal trainer's head backward. Then he turned and raced for his wagon.

"Come back," Gunther shouted after him. "Stay, swine, and fight like a man."

Cimarron ignored him, and when he reached his wagon, he quickly untied his horse and swung into the saddle. Wheeling the black, he raced toward the creek and the loudly bawling cattle that were splashing out of it as they raced north after the lead steers.

He joined several of the cowhands who were also mounted and trying to stop the stampede before it could fully develop into a headlong rush to nowhere.

As he urged the black closer to the lunging bodies of the cattle, he freed the coiled rope that was tied to his saddle horn and, holding it in his left hand, used it to lash the nearest of the cattle, forcing them backward. His tactic succeeded in slowing down some of the animals, but those beyond them passed on.

As he and the cowhands fought to turn them back, the longhorns raced around horses and men, no longer bawling now, intent only on escaping the danger they had become aware of and were apparently determined to put far behind them.

A steer, its head swinging from side to side, abruptly lunged to one side and one of its horns grazed Cimarron's horse, causing it to try to bolt. He gripped the reins tightly, backed the horse up, and when he had it under control again, went racing north as Rhodes, mounted now and riding just ahead of him, yelled, "Turn them back, goddammit, or we'll lose them."

Cimarron outdistanced Rhodes, his boots straining against his stirrups, his body bent forward over his horse's neck as he drove the black as hard as he could in his effort to reach the front of the herd in time to turn it back before any serious damage was done to the stock. He remembered the cattle he had long ago had to shoot after a stampede because of broken legs or because they had gone headlong over a cliff in their frightened flight and, although still alive, would never rise from where they had fallen.

"Get up in front of these beeves," he yelled to a cowhand riding just ahead of him.

"What the hell do you think I'm trying to do?" the man yelled back over his shoulder. "Sprout wings and fly away from here?"

That's maybe not such a bad idea, Cimarron found himself thinking as he brutally lashed the nearest of the longhorns with his rope.

A steer bawled and tossed its head, catching the rope on one of its horns, and then, as the animal raced on, it ripped the rope from Cimarron's hand.

Suddenly, the herd veered to the east for no apparent reason.

"Look out!" Cimarron shouted to warn the cowhand ahead of him as he quickly turned his horse and galloped away from the onrushing herd. He looked back over his shoulder at the sound of the man's sudden scream and he saw the man and his mount go down as the cattle overtook and plowed into them.

He was about to turn his horse to try to save the man, but before he could do so, he realized it was too late for such an attempt.

The lead longhorn's left front hoof came down upon the cowhand's right leg, and the man, his eyes squeezed shut, gave an agonized scream as he struggled valiantly to get to his feet and flee the awful death that was about to overtake him.

He never made it. As the longhorns thundered on, the hapless rider and his mount disappeared from view beneath the mindless hooves of the herd.

As suddenly as the herd had changed course, it did so again, and Cimarron wheeled his horse and went galloping back toward it, grimacing as he rode past the fragments of bone and gobbets of bloodied flesh that had been pounded into the ground, the flesh and blood that had once been a living man and horse and now were nothing but a hopelessly torn and broken horror.

The cattle now were heading northwest and they were sending thick clouds of dust swirling up into the afternoon air as they plunged on.

Cimarron coughed as he rode into the dust, blinked, rode on, his throat parched, his eyes smarting, his body bathed in sweat.

The horse under him stumbled on a stone and almost went down.

He grabbed the saddle horn and held tightly to it to keep from falling, and the black, feeling the reins slacken, turned and headed east, away from the rampaging herd.

Cimarron swore and savagely seized the reins, forcing the black to turn and head back the way it had come. He ignored the bloody saliva that flew in wet strings from the animal's lips as the iron bit cut cruelly into them.

He swore again even more angrily when he saw the herd begin to head down into a gulch and the cowhands closest to the lead steers veer away to keep from entering the gulch as well and possibly finding themselves caught between the walls of the gulch and the bodies of the cattle, where they would be crushed to death.

"Cut the herd in two," he yelled at the top of his voice after seeing how the relatively narrow mouth of the gulch was starting to slow down the stampede.

One of the cowhands gave him a wave and then shouted orders to the other men near him. As they rode forward toward the mouth of the gulch to divide the herd, Cimarron galloped up the steep incline on the eastern side of the entrance to it. When he reached the high ground, he raked his horse with his spurs and the animal sped on toward the distant point where the high ground began to slope down again at the far end of the gulch.

Less than a minute later, he drew rein and then sprang from the saddle. The instant his boots hit the ground he was off and running toward the edge of the cliff. When he reached it, he looked down and then, without breaking stride, went racing along the cliff in a northerly direction.

Moments later, he leaped from the cliff and landed with a body-breaking *thunk* on the back of one of the longhorns that was struggling to fight its way through the gulch, now tightly packed with a roiling sea of cattle.

He grabbed the horns of the animal under him; then, crawling on his hands and knees, he made his way between the horns and up onto the body of the animal in front of him. Then the next. As the heaving flesh beneath him surged, subsided, and then surged again, he halted and held tightly to a steer's horns to keep from going down and under the cattle. He moved on a moment later, the loud clattering of horns ringing in his ears and the strong scent of manure involuntarily dropped by the alarmed animals reeking in his nostrils.

He got to his feet, keenly conscious of the fact that he had to act fast before the leaders of the stampede were able to emerge from the gulch. He ran unsteadily, his arms outstretched to balance himself and with his body swaying and bending first forward and then backward, along the broad backs of the animals; when he was just behind the lead steers, he dropped to his knees again. He reached behind him and pulled his knife from his boot. Leaning forward with the knife gripped firmly in his right hand and holding on to one of the horns of the steer beneath him with his left, he deftly slashed downward, first on one side of the lead steer's head and then on the other. He climbed onto the steer on his left and repeated the bloody process. Then, as he stood up and went hopping from one broad back of the tightly bunched cattle to the next, he used his knife on four more of the lead steers.

The animals bawled their pain and fear as they were forced to slow their headlong flight. One suddenly stopped in its tracks. Then a second steer stopped. The weight of those behind the two who had halted pushed them forward but slowly.

Cimarron, clinging to the horn of the steer under him, wiped his bloody knife on the animal's hide before returning it to his boot. He rode the steer out of the gulch, the animal walking now and bellowing its pain, its head hanging down, the cattle behind it brought almost to a halt by the slow pace of their wounded leaders.

"Form a line across the front of the herd," he shouted to the cowhands who were galloping down the sides of the gulch from the high ground behind them. "Shoot to turn them if they start stampeding again."

As the cattle came out of the gulch, they began to fan out behind their leaders and then they ranged outward on both sides of them. The cowhands began to herd them up onto the high ground and drive them back to their bed-ground.

Cimarron jumped down from the steer he had been riding and quickly backed away from it, in case it decided to try to gore him.

"You blinded them," a furious Rhodes shouted as he rode up to where Cimarron stood sweating and dusty as he watched the cowhands skillfully work the herd. "What a bloody mess you've made of them."

Cimarron, after swallowing hard to try to wash the dust from his mouth and throat, said, "I didn't blind them."

"You did! Look at them. Their eyes are all bloody."

"I just cut the muscles in their upper eyelids so's they'd droop. I didn't cut out their eyes like you're thinking I did. But what I did'll make them blind for a time, not to mention tame. Sooner or later, though, their eyelids'll heal and they'll be able to see again. But they won't be so pretty anymore, on account of their eyelids'll always be a bit droopy from now on. Beef buyers won't mind that fact too much, though. I reckon."

"Where'd you learn to pull a stunt like that?" Rhodes asked.

"I've seen rustlers use it," Cimarron answered. "That's how they steal calves that aren't weaned. They cut their eyelids so they can't find their mamas, and by the time their eyelids are healed, they're weaned and the rustlers go and slap their brand on the young 'uns."

"Mr. Rhodes," one of the cowhands called out from the high ground above the gulch, and when he had the trail boss's attention, he shouted down, "Deke Stover's dead, Mr. Rhodes. He got himself run under by those hell-bent beeves before they went into the gulch down there."

Rhodes acknowledged the news with a frown and a surly curse. "I hate like hell to lose a good man on a drive like this, and Stover was better than good," he said sadly. "Stover came close to being the best man I've ever had working for me."

"You're likely to find out you lost more than a top hand."

Rhodes gave Cimarron an inquiring look.

"When you take a tally of your longhorns, I won't be a bit surprised to learn that you're missing some of them."

"We can round them up, given time."

"Maybe you can and maybe you can't. You know what started that stampede, do you?" When Rhodes shook his head, Cimarron continued, "It was reservation Indians— Apaches. Like as not they were some of the bunch you told me you'd run into back along the trail. I caught sight of them over beyond the creek when the cattle were getting themselves ready to run. They were hunkered down by the herd and waving wolf pelts to spook your critters."

"And spook them they damn well did!" Rhodes exclaimed. "Those heathen redskins. I've got a good mind to get my men and go gunning for them."

"You're welcome to do what you think best, Rhodes, but were I you, I'd leave them be, on account of they just might decide to start shooting back if you go after them. They've most probably got what they came after—beef. Beef you ought to have turned over to them when they asked for it, if I might be so bold as to state my opinion. If you'd've done that, chances are you'd be better off than you are now. You'd be short a few head of stock, but your hand Stover would still be alive and riding for you."

"I don't need any lectures from you, Cimarron. You tend to your business and I'll tend to mine in the way both of us sees fit. But I'll tell you one thing. Nobody steals my beef and gets away with it."

As Rhodes walked away from him, Cimarron began to climb up the side of the gulch, and when he reached the top, he walked on until he finally reached his black, which stood grazing contentedly on the high ground. He examined the wound in the animal's shoulder, which had been made by the horn of one of the steers during the stampede, and was relieved to see that it was shallow and not serious.

He boarded the horse and moved out at a trot, his eyes on the herd in the distance as the cowhands continued moving it south toward the bed-ground beside the creek.

When he reached the camp, he looked around, but Gunther was nowhere in sight.

Mr. Simpson was, and Cimarron rode up to him. "We're moving out of here."

"Now?" Simpson asked, and then pointed to the setting sun. "It will be dark soon."

"Now, Mr. Simpson. The boss of this herd's a bullheaded man, and bullheaded men, I learned a long time ago, can cause trouble for other people, not to mention for themselves. He's talking about going gunning for the Apaches who stampeded his herd. Were I those Apaches, I'd sure enough come gunning right back at him if he does such a foolhardy thing. If that happens, I don't want you or your people—or me neither—to be right in the middle of a small war.

"There's a town called Stony Springs west of us. We ought to be able to get there by morning—late morning. It's real close to the Texas border and it's where I'll be leaving you folks. Might be you can put on a show for the good people of Stony Springs."

"Of course, we shall do that, once we arrive safely. But do you really insist on us moving through the night, Cimarron? It's dangerous. You know what happened to Denton the night we left McAlester."

"I know. But, yes, we'd best be getting out of here. There's Rhodes over there now and it looks to me like he's riling up his men, getting them set on maybe scalping some Apaches."

"We'll pull out, then," Simpson agreed. "I'll be glad to leave those Apaches you just mentioned far behind us. I just hope that the town of Stony Springs doesn't have the equivalent of a Brother Ezra in it who will cause us the kind of trouble that madman did."

"Spread the word, Mr. Simpson. We're moving out."

When Simpson had left him, Cimarron rode over to his wagon, got out of the saddle, and tied his horse behind the wagon.

When Davey appeared a moment later, Cimarron said, "I

153

wonder, boy, if you'd get the gear off my horse. He's all sweaty and blowing hard on account of the way I was just riding him.''

''I'll see to him, Cimarron. Be glad to.''

''Rub him down good. Hang my saddle blanket up on the wagon to dry out.''

As Davey went to the horse, Cimarron climbed into the wagon and threw himself down on the bunk against the wall. He clasped his hands behind his head and lay there on his back, his legs spread, his eyes closed.

But it was not sleep he was seeking. He was seeking answers to the questions that had been forming in his mind ever since his encounter with Deputy Len Henderson and the bank robber Dave Youngman.

The questions kept erupting in his mind until he finally pushed them aside and began to think about other things. He saw in his mind's eye the picture of Lucinda that hung on her wagon's wall. He recalled her having told him that she sold autographed copies of that picture to the townspeople in the interval between the afternoon's menagerie display and the evening's circus performance.

He recalled the fact that Davey had told him that the bank in Paradise had been robbed just before closing time and that Henderson had said that the banks in McAlester and Fort Smith had been robbed at about the same time of day.

He could find no answers to the questions that came swarming back into his mind to buzz there so annoyingly. Neither could he make all the pieces of the puzzle that was bothering him fit neatly together in any meaningful way.

Maybe I'm twisting the tail of the wrong bronc, he thought. Maybe I've just got too much imagination. But, dammit, something just don't sit right with me about this whole bank-robbery business.

He wondered if the town of Stony Springs had a bank. The last time he'd been in the town, it was little more than a cluster of hastily thrown up shacks and a few tents. In one of the tents, a lawyer had set up shop, he recalled, and the man was doing a brisk business settling disputes and leasing land.

But that was more than two years ago, he reminded himself. By now, maybe a banker's come and put down roots in Stony Springs, he speculated.

That's the first thing I got to do, he decided. Find out if there's a bank in Stony Springs. If there is one, well, that might—given time and a little luck—give me the answers to some of these questions that are irking me worse than blowflies irk a cut cow they're feeding on.

10

"Maybe you can tell me something I'd like to know," Cimarron said to Babe Folsom early the following afternoon as they stood together on the circus lot just west of the town of Stony Springs.

"Maybe I can," Babe said with a smile. "I can tell you you're one helluva he-man that's got fur on his brisket. Is that what you had in mind?"

"Nope, but that's a nice thing to hear coming from a lovely lady like yourself. But what I want to know is, does Lucinda draw much of a crowd when she autographs those pictures of hers that she sells after the menagerie display?"

"Does dead meat draw flies?"

"She does, then?"

Babe nodded. "All the men stand around ogling her. The women do, too, for that matter. The men want to have her and the women wish they *were* her. Oh, I'll admit it. I envy her. Hey, where are you going?"

"See you later, Babe." Cimarron gave her a wave as he sprinted toward his wagon. When he reached it, he boarded his horse and rode into Stony Springs.

He asked the first person he met if there was a bank in town, and when he had been told that there was and had been given directions to it, he rode down the main street until he reached it.

Once inside the bank, he asked for the man in charge, and

when the bank's owner had been pointed out to him, he went up to the man and said, "My name's Cimarron and I'm a deputy marshal out of Fort Smith."

"You want to open an account with us, do you, Deputy?" inquired the bank manager. "My name is O'Day and I'm at your service, sir."

"I don't want to open an account, Mr. O'Day. What I want is for you to listen to what I'm going to tell you, and listen real careful."

"Oh, dear!" O'Day exclaimed at one point as Cimarron explained why he had come to the bank. "Oh, my, may the saints in heaven preserve us!" he cried when Cimarron had finished speaking.

"It's not the saints that'll be preserving you, Mr. O'Day," Cimarron said grimly. "If it turns out that there's any preserving to do, I'll be the one to do it. That's why I'm here."

"What are you planning to do?"

"I was just about to tell you that."

Late that same afternoon, Cimarron returned to the bank after having finished a leisurely meal of steak and boiled potatoes at a combination restaurant and saloon in the center of town.

He took up his prearranged position at a small desk across the room from the barred tellers' cages, pulled his stetson down low on his forehead, picked up a pencil, and began to doodle on a piece of paper.

He was drawing a naked woman with pendulous breasts when the man he had been expecting rode up outside the bank, dismounted, and then, crouching behind his horse, tied a bandanna around the lower half of his face.

Cimarron lowered his head and appeared to be concentrating on the paper lying before him on the desk, and when the masked man entered the bank, his gun drawn, and shouted "Customers on the floor facedown—move it!" he knocked over his chair in his haste to hit the floor.

"This gunnysack," the masked man barked to one of the

tellers, "is empty. I want it filled fast with cash—folding money only, no coins."

Cimarron raised his head slightly at the sound of the familiar voice so that he could see the bank robber. His hand snaked down along his hip and came to rest on the butt of his Colt.

When the robber reached for the gunnysack, which had been filled with money by the trembling teller, Cimarron made his move. Without rising from his supine position, he unleathered his revolver and, holding it in both hands with his elbows propped on the wooden floor, said, "Get rid of that gun."

The robber, instead of obeying the order, fired at Cimarron, who, because he had been expecting just that to happen, was rolling to one side before the bullet left the masked man's gun. Then he too fired, and his shot slammed into the robber's left shoulder.

As the masked man cried out in pain and involuntarily turned sideways, Cimarron sprang to his feet and lunged forward to rip the gun from the would-be bandit's hand.

"Oh, my goodness," moaned Mr. O'Day, who was lying nearby. "Is it all over?"

"It's over for you," Cimarron said to the man he had shot in the shoulder as he shoved the man's gun into his waistband. He reached out and pulled down the bandit's bandanna so that it hung loosely around his neck. Then he took the gunnysack from his captive's hand and returned it to the nervous teller.

"You can all get up now," he told the customers and Mr. O'Day, who were littering the floor of the bank. "You can all go on about your business now without further trouble from this jasper. Him and me, we're leaving."

Cimarron prodded the man, who was staring at him with an expression of utter surprise on his face, and then he turned and walked out of the bank with Cimarron right behind him.

"Where are you taking me?" the man asked, his hands held high above his head.

Cimarron told him.

*   *   *

As Cimarron rode onto the circus lot behind his prisoner, Matt Ledman came out from behind the cage that held Gunther's lion, Caesar, and stopped in his tracks.

"Where the hell have you been?" he barked at the man with Cimarron. "It's damn nearly time to get ready for tonight's performance. I figured you'd be late again the same way you were back in Paradise. And in McAlester too."

"He won't be in the show tonight, Ledman," Cimarron said, and then ordered the man in front of him to dismount. "If Tinker here's going to give any shows," he said as Ramona started to pass him, her eyes on the ground, "he'll be giving them behind bars."

Ramona halted and looked up at him. "What are you talking about, Cimarron?" Her gaze shifted to Tinker Sloan, who stood with one hand on his saddle horn beside the horse he had been riding.

"Tinker just did some clowning around in Stony Springs," Cimarron told her. "At the bank there. He tried to rob it." He glanced past Ledman to where Lucinda stood smiling and signing photographs in front of the grind-show tent.

"You're crazy, lawman," Ledman said angrily. "Tinker's no bank robber."

As Lucinda looked up and saw Cimarron, he touched the brim of his hat to her.

But her eyes were on Tinker. She hurried away from the crowd around her as if responding to the doleful expression that had settled on Tinker's face.

"What's going on?" she inquired of Cimarron as she came up to stand in front of him. "Is anything wrong?"

Cimarron got out of the saddle and said, "You could say that, yes. I caught Tinker trying to rob the bank in town. Tinker, let's go." He pointed.

"You're going to lock me in there with Caesar?" Tinker asked uneasily. "Don't do that, Deputy. I'm deathly afraid of those big cats of Gunther's."

"You'll have that partition in between the two of you," Cimarron responded as he took the cage key from his pocket.

159

After he had locked Tinker in the safety cage, he returned to Lucinda and the others and was joined a moment later by Babe.

"Everybody looks like their favorite dog just died," Babe commented. "What's wrong?"

Cimarron told her.

"Are you sure, Cimarron?" she asked, and glanced at the caged Tinker.

"I'm sure. I caught him red-handed."

"You just happened to be in the bank at the time?" Ledman asked suspiciously.

"Nope. I went there on purpose. I figured it was about to be robbed today since you circus folks will be heading west after tonight's show."

"You suspected that Tinker would try to rob the bank?" Ramona asked breathlessly.

"I did."

"But *why* did you?" Lucinda asked, frowning. "I mean, what in the world would make you suspect Tinker of planning to rob the bank?"

"Because of a few things I heard and saw and some I just thought of," Cimarron answered. "To start with, when I first thought back to what Deputy Henderson had told me about the banks being robbed in McAlester and Fort Smith, it struck me that this circus was in those towns at the times those two banks were looted."

"But that might have been just a coincidence," Ramona pointed out.

"Thought the same thing myself at first," Cimarron acknowledged. "But it nagged at me—the way Youngman claimed he was innocent of those robberies."

"You believed him?" Ledman asked, incredulity evident in his tone of voice. "I heard Deputy Henderson say that witnesses had identified Youngman as the bank robber in both of those towns."

"Henderson said that, all right," Cimarron agreed. "So I was stumped for a spell. Until I thought about how Youngman

160

had looked so familiar to me, only I couldn't remember ever meeting up with the man. You folks—do you happen, any of you, to remember what Youngman looked like?''

"I do," Ramona said. "He was short. He had blond hair—blond curly hair.''

"He was on the fat side," Ledman volunteered. "Paunchy." Cimarron pointed to Tinker.

Ramona gasped.

Lucinda said, "So that's why you thought you'd seen Youngman before. Because—''

"Because he comes close to being a dead ringer for Tinker Sloan," Cimarron interrupted. "Then there was the matter of Youngman swearing he wouldn't be caught dead wearing a derby hat, but Henderson said that witnesses said that the bank robber wore a bandanna and a derby hat. That stuck in my craw, though for a while I didn't know why. But then I remembered the day I first met Tinker back in Fort Smith—the day you introduced me to him, Lucinda. I remembered he was wearing a derby that day, and remembering that, it began to seem to me that maybe Youngman had been telling Henderson the truth all along about him being innocent. Especially when I made the connection between Youngman and Tinker—thought about how the two of them could be cousins if not brothers, considering they look so similar.

"It started to seem to me that the witnesses to the bank robberies in McAlester and Fort Smith could have been mistaken. You look at a man with a bandanna covering half of his face and his hat pulled down low, and if that man's built a lot like another man, if he has the same kind and color hair as that other man—well, I guess you can see how the land started to lie in my mind at the time. I could understand how those witnesses would point the finger straight at Youngman. Well, then I came up with a way to find out if the circus—somebody in it—might maybe be the real robber.''

"A way?" Babe asked hesitantly. "What way?''

"I remembered Henderson telling me that neither he nor Youngman had been anywhere near Paradise. So I sent Davey

Corliss into Paradise and he found out, damned if he didn't, that the bank there had been robbed during the time we—this circus—was there. He found out it'd been robbed just before closing time, like the other two were. He found out that the robber was wearing a derby hat and a bandanna around his face."

"So you knew it was Tinker," Lucinda said, and glanced in the man's direction.

"Not then, I didn't. Not for sure, anyway. But Davey got a pretty fair description of the robber and it sure did sound a lot like Tinker. But the clincher—" Cimarron indicated Tinker's gun in his waistband. "The clincher was this gun. Davey found out that the robber had been toting a Navy Colt. This gun's a Navy Colt. I took it from Tinker in Stony Springs."

"You said the banks were robbed around closing time," Babe said softly. "Tinker went into those three towns when they were about empty because most of the townies were on our lot." She let out a little cry. "That's why you asked me before if Lucinda drew a crowd after the menagerie display, isn't it, Cimarron?"

"It is. The strays hung around her and that kept Tinker from taking the risk of finding too many people in the banks, one or more of whom might cause him trouble. Well, the next thing for me to do was clear to me by that time."

"You went into Stony Springs," Ledman said. "To the bank there."

"I did and, lo and behold, along came Tinker right on schedule."

"He's wounded," Babe said sorrowfully.

"You shot him, Cimarron?" Lucinda asked excitedly, her eyes beginning to glitter.

He turned away from her without answering her question.

"What are you going to do now?" Ledman asked him.

"Try to find the money Tinker stole. You'll maybe remember that Henderson thought Youngman had not only stolen it but had gone and hidden it somewhere. He didn't. Tinker did."

Once inside Tinker's wagon, Cimarron stood and looked around, wondering where the man might have hidden the money he had stolen. He decided to start his search with the four-drawer wooden dresser that stood against one wall. He searched through each of its drawers but found only clothes, a makeup kit, old magazines, and an empty sack of Bull Durham tobacco.

Next, he tried the trunk that sat on the floor beside the dresser. More clothes. Costumes. Circus posters with pictures of Tinker in full clown regalia on them. As he disgustedly slammed the trunk's lid shut, Davey appeared in the doorway.

"Miss Folsom told me you were in here, Cimarron. Did you find the money?"

"Nope." Cimarron looked around and then felt beneath the table and under the seats of the two wooden chairs flanking it.

"I'll help you look," Davey volunteered and upended a coffee can that sat on a wall shelf; it turned out to be empty. Then he took a wooden cigar box down from the shelf and opened it. "Nothing in here but old photographs of Tinker," he stated.

Cimarron lifted the lid of a cracker barrel that sat in one corner of the wagon and found it empty. He replaced the lid and turned to find that Davey had disappeared. He shrugged and continued searching the wagon. When, after he had gone through everything in it, including Tinker's bunk, he left the wagon and went outside to find Davey crawling out from under it, an oilcloth-covered bundle in one hand.

"This might be it, Cimarron. I just found it roped to the bottom of the wagon."

Cimarron took the bundle from him and opened it. He stared down at the money it contained for a moment and then, tossing the oilcloth aside, began to count it.

"Just over two thousand dollars," he said when he had completed his count. He recalled asking Henderson how much money had been stolen from the banks in Fort Smith and McAlester. Close to five thousand dollars from the Fort

Smith bank, he remembered Henderson saying. And over seven thousand from the bank in McAlester. Now where, he wondered, is the rest of the loot from those two banks, plus the one in Paradise? "Davey, take another look under the wagon. There's a whole pile of stolen money still missing."

Davey disappeared and then quickly reappeared, shaking his head. "There's nothing else under there, Cimarron."

Cimarron pocketed the money and started to walk away, but when Davey called out to him, he halted and turned around.

"I almost forgot, Cimarron. Mr. Kleist, he said he heard you were back from town and he told me to tell you he wants to talk to you. He said you could find him in the big top."

"Did he say what he wanted to talk to me about?"

"No. But he sounded awful mad about something."

Cimarron, leaving Davey behind, headed for the big top, and once within it, he found Gunther moving about inside the barred arena where he worked his cats. Cimarron strode toward the arena, and when he reached it, he stepped inside it and stood watching in silence as Gunther busied himself with the huge hoops he used in his act, the ones he set afire and forced his cats to jump through.

When Gunther had finished coating them with tallow and had hung them on an iron hook protruding from one of the bars, he turned and saw Cimarron watching him.

"You have the key to Caesar's cage," he said bluntly, and held out his hand. "I want it."

"I'm not giving it to you, Gunther."

Gunther's eyes narrowed and his outstretched hand fell to his side. "I must bring Caesar here to the arena. I must teach him—"

"Maybe you heard that I'm using part of Caesar's cage for a jail, Gunther."

"I heard, yes."

"For you to get Caesar out of his cage, you'd first have to let Tinker out of it and I'm not having that, on account of

Tinker might make a break for it and I'd have to chase—maybe shoot—him, neither of which I want to do. So the cage key stays with me till you people move out for the Texas line tonight and I start back to Fort Smith with my prisoner.''

Gunther, his face darkening, strode past Cimarron and out of the arena. Suddenly, he turned, slammed the barred door shut, and quickly locked it with a key he took from his pocket.

Then, returning the key to his pocket, he said, "I go now to find the gaffer. You—you will stay in that cage like the wild beast you are until I return with Mr. Simpson. Maybe he can make you surrender my key. Maybe he can force you to stop making trouble for us. I hope he will send you away from us.''

Cimarron walked over to the arena's locked door and gripped two of its bars in his hands. "Gunther, I'm a reasonable man most of the time, but I can be troublesome when I'm crossed. Now, you let me out of here and I'll try hard to forget that you're one irksome son of a bitch, not to mention a powerful pain in the ass.''

"Throw my key through the bars. Then I will let you out.''

Cimarron slowly and wordlessly shook his head.

"I warn you, Cimarron. I will find a way to fix you and fix you good!'' Gunther turned on his heels and walked out of the big top.

Cimarron watched him go. He saw him stop as Lucinda passed the entrance, and speak to her before turning and pointing at him. He heard Gunther laugh, but he noticed that Lucinda didn't.

When the pair separated and moved off in different directions, to disappear from view, he turned and studied the arena, his glance roving from the hoops hanging on their iron hook to the whip lying in the tanbark near the gate of the chute through which the cats were sent into the arena and then onto the gaily painted stools that were piled on top of one another on the far side of the arena.

He looked up. The top of those bars, he thought, must be

nine feet or more above me. He looked down at the iron band that encircled the bars parallel to the ground. He tentatively thrust a boot between the bars and then, when it slid easily between them, he looked up again briefly before suddenly leaping from the ground and grabbing the bars. He held tightly to them and began to pull his body upward, struggling to place his boots on the iron band encircling the bars.

The dull sound of wood scraping against wood came to him and he looked down but saw nothing. He looked around, but there was no one in the big top with him.

He swore as he lost his grip on the bars and dropped down to the ground. He stood there for a moment, rubbing his sweating palms to dry them on his jeans, and then he crouched and made ready to spring upward again and make another try at climbing over the tops of the bars and out of Gunther's arena.

A throaty mutter off to his left made him turn his head and his body went suddenly stiff as he saw what had made the sound. A leopard, its belly brushing the tanbark-covered ground, was coming through the slatted wooden chute toward the arena, and as it moved lithely forward, another low mutter, a subdued snarl, issued from its open mouth.

The stiffness left Cimarron's body and he sprinted forward toward the open mouth of the chute, reaching up desperately to release the raised barrier above the chute's open gate.

He had his hand on it and was about to free it and send it slamming down to block the leopard from entering the arena, when the cat sprang forward and, with one swift downward swipe of its right paw, clawed Cimarron's left thigh, ripping his jeans and his flesh as it did so.

He let go of the gate's barrier and hurriedly backed away from the chute's entrance as the leopard entered the arena and rose to its full height.

It stood its ground, watching Cimarron, its ears laid back against its tawny skull, its eyes wide and cruelly gleaming.

Cimarron's gaze flicked from the animal to a second leopard that was leaving the chute and crawling into the arena to take up a position to the right of and just behind the first one. He eased slowly to one side, aware of the four yellow eyes that moved with him as they kept him in their line of vision.

He had the abrupt impulse to yell for Gunther to come and help him as pain pulsed his wounded leg, but he didn't act upon it. That bastard, he thought. He's gone and done what he said he was going to do. Fix me, and fix me good. I'll get no help from him.

As the leopard closer to him took a tentative step in his direction, Cimarron halted, bent down, seized Gunther's whip from the ground, and lashed out with it at the leopard facing him.

The leather savagely slashed the animal's spotted flank, causing it to snarl and then to scream. The leopard behind it backed away and then bellied down to lie growling on the ground.

Holding the whip high above his head, Cimarron moved slowly to his right, the muted growling of the two leopards a lethal litany in his ears.

He had almost reached the stack of painted stools that Gunther used in his act when the leopard he had lashed with the whip sprang at him. He snapped the whip and it caught the animal on the shoulders, but it failed to stop its spring.

Cimarron swiftly leaped to the side and the leopard landed just beyond him. It slowly turned toward him, its sharp white teeth bared and dripping saliva. Keeping his eyes on it, Cimarron took another step and then another. When the stools were within his reach, he seized one and placed it on the ground beside the arena's bars. Then he placed a second stool on top of the first and climbed up on it. As he stared down at the leopard that had attacked him, he turned, intending to climb up and over the bars.

He saw the second leopard rapidly rise and come racing toward him. It sprang and the stools beneath his boots toppled. As he fell, the leopard's claws shredded his shirt and left bloody and painful trails on the flesh of his chest. He kicked out both booted feet, which landed hard against the gut of the leopard who had been about to claw him a second time. His maneuver lifted the animal off the ground and hurled it some distance away.

He sprang to his feet as the leopard that had first attacked him began to move slowly toward him from the opposite direction. With his head swiveling from side to side to keep both snarling cats in his line of vision, he lashed out again with the whip. But his action served only to anger the leopard that was stalking him. It raised a huge paw and knocked the whip out of his hand.

He hurriedly backed up until his body struck the bars, his head still swiveling, his thoughts racing as he sought a way to save himself from the leopards who were both moving toward him now, their heads lowered and their mouths gaping.

They sprang at him almost simultaneously, and as they did, he hit the ground and scrambled forward. Their powerful lunges carried them over him. He heard them crash into the bars behind him, and then he was up and running, one hand rummaging frantically in his pocket. When he reached the far side of the arena, he took down, using his left hand, one of Gunther's greased hoops from the iron hook on which it was hanging and, with his right, scraped the wooden match he had pulled from his pocket along the sole of his boot.

It flared and he held it to the hoop, which burst into bright dancing flames. He swore and dropped it when the flames seared his hand. But he swiftly retrieved it and held it by the short handle he hadn't noticed before. Then, waving the blazing hoop in a wide arc in front of him, he began a slow and steady advance on the two leopards, who had recovered themselves and were again stalking him.

They halted and began to back away from him and the deadly fire he carried.

He moved closer to them and then to one side of them. Continuing his advance on the growling cats, he managed to maneuver them close to the chute. Still waving the fiery hoop in front of him, he continued to move in their direction, and as he did so, the leopards continued to retreat. When he had them in what he believed was the right position, he suddenly let out a loud yell and brandished the burning hoop directly in front of their faces.

The leopards turned and fled, battling each other as each of them fought to be the first to enter the chute and escape the fire they so desperately feared.

Snapping savagely at its companion, one of the leopards succeeded in entering the chute. The other quickly followed it.

Cimarron ran forward, freed the gate, and slammed it down to block the mouth of the chute. His heart pounding and his breath coming in short painful gasps, he dropped the hoop, stamped out its flames, and then reached out and grasped the bars with both hands. He hung there against them, his body limp, his right cheek pressed against the cold iron.

The scream of a man that came from somewhere beyond the big top caused him to jerk upright and let go of the bars.

He ran back to the pile of stools, and placing one upon the other as he had done before, he climbed up on them, gripped the bars, and hauled himself up until his boots rested on the iron band encircling the arena.

Minutes later, he was over the top of the bars and on the ground outside the arena. He turned away from it and raced toward the big top's entrance.

As he emerged from the big top, his shirt and one leg of his jeans in tatters, he saw people running out of the cook tent and climbing down from their wagons to halt, horrified, as they, like him, saw Caesar straddling and attacking Tinker Sloan, who was screaming in terror as he tried to battle the beast that was savagely biting and clawing him.

"The partition's gone," somebody cried.

Cimarron sprinted toward the cage, which was no longer divided in half, unleathering his Colt as he did so. He was halfway to it when he came to an abrupt halt. He raised his revolver and took aim.

"Don't kill him," Lucinda cried as she ran toward him.

He fired before she could come between him and his intended target.

As his bullet slammed into Caesar's body, the lion let out a loud roar that blended eerily with Tinker's anguished screams.

Cimarron, cocking his gun, watched the lion's body convulse and then seem to turn in upon itself as blood from the bullet wound in its side spurted out to stain the bars of its cage. He held his fire as Caesar, a kind of soft keening coming from his throat, collapsed on Tinker's torn and mangled body below him.

Cimarron, blood running down his chest and leg, ran to the cage wagon and swiftly unlocked the door of the cage. He dragged Tinker out from beneath Caesar's corpse and placed the man on his back on the ground as a crowd, which included Lucinda and Gunther, gathered around him.

"Did anybody see what happened here?" Cimarron asked without taking his eyes from Tinker's mutilated body. "Did anybody see who pulled that partition out?"

No one had.

Tinker stirred. He groaned and then opened the one eye that Caesar had not clawed from its socket. When he saw Cimarron, his lips parted.

Cimarron, as Tinker struggled to speak, got down on his knees beside the obviously dying man and bent his head to hear what Tinker was trying to tell him.

Tinker's words, spaced far apart and slurred, caused him to look up at the faces peering down at him. Later, as Tinker stopped speaking and his body suddenly stiffened, he looked down again. When Tinker's body relaxed and his single remaining eye glazed, he rose and yelled, "Davey!"

When Davey had forced his way through the shocked crowd of circus people, Cimarron took him aside and gave him an order.

As Davey went racing away, Cimarron watched Gunther climb into the cage, kneel down, and cradle Caesar's huge head in his arms as tears spilled from his eyes and ran down his cheeks.

Cimarron stepped up to the cage and said, "I owe you an apology, Gunther, for what I've been thinking about you." When Gunther glanced over his shoulder at him, Cimarron continued, "I thought it was you who let those leopards into the arena to try to make a meal of me."

"What are you talking about?" Gunther, a frown on his wet face, asked.

Cimarron told him what had just happened in the arena.

"Do you know who let my two leopards out of their cage?" Gunther asked when he had finished.

"I know."

"Who did it?"

Instead of answering, Cimarron gazed off into the distance in search of Davey, but the boy was nowhere in sight. He turned back to the anxious faces watching him and spoke to Lucinda. "You thought I was going to kill Tinker?"

"No," she said, shaking her head. "I thought you were going to shoot Caesar and I tried to stop you. He is—he was a very valuable animal. I knew you weren't going to shoot Tinker."

Cimarron was about to say something more to her when Davey came running up to him and thrust an oilcloth-covered bundle into his hands.

"It was where you said it would probably be, Cimarron," Davey declared breathlessly.

Cimarron opened the bundle and counted the money it contained before handing it back to Davey. "You guard that money for me, boy, for the time being." As Davey stuffed the bundle inside his shirt, Cimarron said, addressing the silent crowd, "Tinker told me who pulled out the partition so that Caesar could kill him."

A hushed murmur raced through the crowd.

"He also told me why it was done. Seems Tinker was head over heels in love. Had been, I gather, for a long time. But he wasn't loved back, sad to say. So he figured out a way to maybe buy the love he couldn't get any other way. He started

171

robbing banks and turning most of the money he stole over to the one he loved, keeping only some of it for himself.

"But when I caught him robbing the bank in Stony Springs, the one he loved figured he might tell who else was involved in those robberies as an accessory of sorts. Now, Tinker thought he was about to become a free man when he saw his accomplice, who wanted the money he stole and not him, turn two of Gunther's leopards into the chute that led into the arena where Gunther had gone and locked me up.

"Turns out Tinker was wrong, though. His loved one went and turned on him next, just to make sure to keep herself out of jail in case I managed to get away from those leopards she set on me. The lady waited till the coast was clear and then she pulled out the partition, letting Caesar get to Tinker."

"What lady?" Babe Folsom asked from the edge of the crowd.

"Well, Babe," he said, "maybe 'lady's' the wrong word to use in this case. But before I answer your question, I've got to tell you all that I knew Tinker had told me the truth when Davey Corliss found the rest of the loot he had stolen tied under one of the circus wagons."

"Which wagon?" Gunther asked as he climbed down from the cage wagon, Caesar's blood on his clothes.

"Hers," Cimarron said, spinning around and pointing at Lucinda.

As she turned and tried to flee, he reached out and seized her by the arm. "Gunther, you get your dead lion out of that wagon."

When Gunther had done so and after he had placed Caesar's corpse beside the equally lifeless body of Tinker, Cimarron thrust Lucinda into the blood-drenched cage and locked the padlock on its door.

"Damn you, Cimarron!" she snarled, reminding him of Caesar.

"What will you do with her?" Gunther asked him.

"I'll be taking her back to Fort Smith to stand trial for attempting to murder me and for murdering Tinker with deadly weapons—namely, Caesar and your two leopards. I'll hang on to the key to that cage awhile longer, if you've no objections."

"Welcome you are to it."

Cimarron pocketed the key and said, "Gunther, I'm as unhappy as a man in hell on a hot day that I had to shoot your lion to try to save Tinker."

"I know you had to do it." Gunther looked up at Lucinda.

"She's one wild animal even you couldn't tame, Gunther," Cimarron remarked. "You're better off without her, believe me."

"I know now that you are right." Gunther looked down at the dead Tinker.

Cimarron took a step backward and beckoned. When Ramona stepped forward, he led her up to Gunther. "This lady's not likely to try to have you torn to bits if what you do or become don't suit her. This lady's likely to— Well, I guess I ought to let her speak on that score for herself."

Mr. Simpson stepped out of the crowd and said to Cimarron, "I wish— You wouldn't want to accompany us all the way to California by any chance, would you, Cimarron?"

Cimarron shook his head and then Simpson's hand. "The Texas border is less than a mile west of here. My assistant deputy United States marshal'll look out for you folks the rest of the way. Won't you, Davey?"

"I'll do my best, Mr. Simpson," Davey promised, his face one huge smile. "But my best won't come even close to Cimarron's."

"You'll do fine, Davey," Cimarron assured him, and then, as Mr. Simpson and the others began to drift away to get ready for the night's performance, he looked down at his bloody torso and leg. And then up, as he felt a soft hand come to rest on his arm, into Babe's solemn face.

"You won't be performing in that roper act tonight," she stated flatly. "And I won't be appearing in the grind show either. I'm going to borrow some of Gunther's tincture of nicotine. You're going to take some and then I'll try to heal your hurts."

"No tincture of nicotine," Cimarron said, shaking his head and placing an arm around her shoulders. "I don't want to be so doped up that I can't appreciate your caring for me."

"And I do intend to care for you, Cimarron," she assured him.

"After you've done that," he said, "I'm taking you into town and we're going to a real nice restaurant I was in before I laid my loop on Tinker and we're going to have us a real fine meal together with all the fancy trimmings just like I promised you we'd do sometime."

"And after that—you'll be leaving us?"

"Nope. Not right away I won't. Not if you'll be kind enough to let me stay the night with you in your wagon."

"I'll let you. Oh, will I ever let you!"

Cimarron and Babe, both of them laughing happily, walked past the caged and angry-eyed Lucinda as they made their merry way toward Babe's wagon.

SPECIAL PREVIEW

Here is the first chapter
from

CIMARRON
IN NO MAN'S LAND

eighth in the new action-packed
CIMARRON series from Signet

1

When the rifle shot sounded and the bullet came keening past
and uncomfortably close to his right ear, Cimarron sprang from
his saddle and dived behind a jagged pile of ice-cracked rubble.

He quickly drew his Colt, cocked it, and squinted up at the
spot from which the shot had come. He blinked, his eyes
dazzled by the reflection of the sun from the starkly white
gypsum-capped peaks of the Glass Mountains through which
he had been riding. He saw nothing except the sun's shimmer-
ing glare.

He glanced to the left up the narrow trail he had been
traveling, which was bordered by a rocky wall and below which
lay a deep ravine. No boulders or rocks littered it. He looked to
the right where the part of the trail he had already traversed
sloped downward and then around the curved side of the rock
wall and out of sight.

That way back there'd be best, he thought. Maybe I can make
it around that bend without getting my ass shot off along the way.

His black pawed the rocky ground and then stamped its feet to rid its hocks of the flies that had been aroused from hibernation by the surprisingly warm sun of the late-March morning.

He gave a low whistle, but the horse ignored him. He swore and damned himself for being five times a fool.

Should have known, he thought. Should damned well have known Steen'd try a trick like this. He's been a bushwhacker practically forever.

He pulled his hat down low on his forehead to shield his eyes from the sun glinting off the white peaks towering above him, and then he swore out loud as a bullet struck the rocks behind which he was crouching and sent a spray of stone dust flying into his face.

He fired at the spot where he had seen the flame spurt from Steen's rifle barrel and a moment later another bullet crashed into his rocky breastwork.

His horse nickered and tossed its head.

Got to get the hell out of here, he thought. Got to try moving down there along my backtrail and then get on up to higher ground, else Steen's liable to pull the selfsame stunt first and put a bullet in my back from higher up, where these rocks won't hide me from him. But how the hell am I to manage that maneuver, considering that, should I show so much as a toe, Steen'll blast me with that rifle he's aiming at me? His gaze swerved back to his horse and then to his '73 Winchester in its saddle boot. Now that's what I'm in sore need of at the moment, he thought. A gun that's got some range to it. My Colt's next door to useless in this fix I'm in.

He stared at the sloping side of the ravine opposite him, which was terraced with blocks and slabs of rock that had been rounded by ice over many years. Green patches of club mosses grew among the rocks. On his side there was a similar but much steeper drop to the bottom of the ravine, which was, he estimated, a good three hundred yards below him.

He slowly eased to his right, careful to keep himself below the uneven crest of the pile of rubble, and then, bellying down on the ground, he began to crawl toward the spot where his backtrail turned south, damning Steen as he went. High ground, he kept repeating to himself as he crawled along crabwise. That's where I've got to get myself to. Maybe then I can find a way to force Steen out into the open and maybe get close enough to him to kill the bastard.

He halted, freezing in place, as a rifle shot rang out and echoed among the mountain peaks.

Who the hell's Steen shooting at now? he wondered. That shot went way behind where I'm at now. He remained motionless, uncertain of Steen's strategy, certain only that the man would kill him if he had the chance to do so and vowing that he would not let Steen achieve his bloody goal, vowing too that he would get the man he had been trailing for more than a week now. The man named Lyle Steen. The man who had brutally raped his own ten-year-old daughter, the child of his common-law marriage to a woman named Bess Aiken.

He crawled on, and when he reached a spot where the rocky wall on his right gave way to a sloping grade, he turned, rose, and then swiftly ran, crouching low, up the slope until he reached a blunt outcropping of rock. He rounded it and ran past stunted pin oaks that were trying their best to grow on the shady north side of the peak. He continued climbing for several minutes and then stopped. He lay bellydown on an upward-angling slab of rock for a moment and then cautiously eased forward. He removed his stetson and peered over the edge of the slab and down at the opposite side of the ravine, trying to spot Steen. He saw no sign of the man.

He cocked his Colt and squeezed the trigger, hoping that his shot would cause Steen to fire up at him and thus reveal his present position.

Steen promptly fired from the opposite side of the ravine.

So he's switched to higher ground too, Cimarron thought as he clapped his hat back on his head and the smoke from Steen's rifle dissipated. Now what in God's name is he shooting at? Not at me, that's for certain. He aimed far too low if it's me he's still trying to take, and he must have seen where my shot came from. But he aimed down there at the spot where I was before. Makes no kind of sense. Not to me, it don't.

He looked down, and then, as another of Steen's rifle shots shredded the silence, he had his answer. He let out an involuntary cry of dismay as he saw his black far below him go racing up the narrow trail. It's my horse he's after, he thought. He's trying to shoot my black, damn his eyes!

He squeezed off another shot, knowing it would neither reach Steen opposite him nor deter the man from trying to bring down the horse.

Flame flashed from the peak opposite Cimarron and below

177

him his horse screamed. It wheeled as if to turn back, reared, and then, with blood streaming from the hole in the right side of its skull, fell backward, lost its footing, and went over the side of the ravine to fall, turning and twisting, down to the bottom of the ravine. It lay there unmoving among the boulders covering the ground beneath its broken body.

Cimarron stared down at the obviously dead animal, almost unaware of Steen's raucous laughter, which suddenly filled the air and went echoing off the peaks of the mountains to blend with its original source, a sound both ghostlike and faintly obscene.

He tore his eyes away from his horse and felt rage rising within him, heating his face and body and forcing furious words from his lips.

"Steen, damn you!" he roared, and his words bounced back at him.

Damnyou, damnyou, damnyou . . .

"I'll get you," he shouted. "If it takes my last breath and my last bullet, I'll get you, Steen."

Steen, steen, steen, steen . . .

Steen's coarse laughter boomed among the echoes.

And then it abruptly died.

Cimarron saw him move out from behind a loblolly pine, his rifle cradled in his right arm. He saw Steen's triumphant smile and he quickly and angrily fired at the man, wanting to wipe his smile off the face of the world while knowing full well that his target was well out of range. He saw Steen disappear and then reappear aboard the dapple he had been riding during his flight. He heard him shout with undisguised glee. "You'll have hell on your hands if you try following me on foot, deputy, because I'm heading all the way to No Man's Land."

Cimarron watched as Steen reined the dapple around and rode slowly down the steep slope; then he stood up, holstering his gun, and made his way back the way he had come. When he reached the mountain trail, he stared down into the ravine for a moment at his dead black. Then he started following the trail back to where it began to rise from the grasslands in the south.

It took him nearly an hour to reach a point where he could safely climb down into the ravine and almost the same amount of time to double back to the spot where his horse lay dead. When he reached the animal, he stared down at it in disbelief.

Its body had been stripped.

His gear was gone—all of it. His saddle, bridle, slicker, and bedroll. His saddlebags, in which he had kept his money and the dried meat of a kit fox he had killed back along the trail. His rifle.

He looked up at the sloping wall of the ravine on his right. Steen, he thought. He wasn't content with just killing my mount. He rode down here before I could get back and he stole my tack, my money, and my rifle.

He swore almost inaudibly and then walked around the horse and, his expression grim, began to make his way north through the ravine, his high-heeled boots already beginning to hurt his feet.

When he came out of the ravine, the sun was approaching its meridian and the wind had risen and was sweeping toward him out of the northwest.

Above him snow geese soared south, their bodies bright white against the cobalt blue of the sky as they flew south after wintering near the Arctic Circle to spend the coming summer in Mexico.

He halted and stood gazing at the surrounding countryside. There was a forest just ahead of him and to the south and north of it were savannas interrupted in places by woodlands.

No Man's Land.

Steen's words echoed in his ears as he considered his next move.

To the west of him was the Cheyenne and Arapaho Reservation. I could maybe buy a horse there on credit, he thought. Give the agent a voucher he can send to Fort Smith for reimbursement. He glanced in that direction.

And then he looked to the north, where the Cherokee Outlet was located. He knew there were scattered cattle ranches in the Outlet that were owned by white men down from Kansas who willingly paid the grazing fees levied by Cherokee Nation. Would one of those ranchers, he wondered, be willing to sell me a horse on credit and maybe get paid for it by the court as much as six months later? Not likely, he decided.

An image of Steen's ten-year-old daughter suddenly loomed large in his mind. Eyes wide and unblinking. Arms hanging limp and stick-thin by her sides. Mute since the day three weeks earlier when Steen had violated her.

The child was joined in Cimarron's mind by her mother, drab

and weary but with a hot fire in her eyes as she testified before the grand jury and told, in plain and ugly words, how Steen had abused her and how she had let him abuse her, fearing that if she didn't submit to his twisted demands he would turn to their daughter and . . .

The day he did—the day, she said, she finally fought back against him to save the child, the fire that now blazed in her eyes had been kindled and she had taken the child, who was suffering from shock, and come to Fort Smith to accuse her common-law husband of his "crime against nature," as she had called it in her grief-stricken testimony.

Sheen's remembered laughter abruptly banished the two images from Cimarron's mind and then the laughter drifted away.

He began walking in a northwesterly direction, the wind lifting his long hair and rippling the fringes on the arms and shoulders of his buckskin jacket.

The sun was on its way down when he spotted the snow-shoe rabbits in the distance.

Three of them. Two of them were fighting over a female, who squatted with apparent unconcern not far from them. All of them were speckled now because their white winter coats were beginning to turn to the brown they wore in summer.

He moved cautiously and noiselessly toward them, unleathering his Colt as he did so. He kept his eyes on the two battling males as he continued moving toward them and the pair continued to attack each other. Then one of them, defeated in his amorous quest, went bounding away to the west, its large hind feet hitting the ground in front of its smaller front ones as it made its escape.

Cimarron dropped down behind a rotting deadfall, and then, after gripping the butt of his Colt with both hands, he steadied it on the tree trunk, took aim, and fired.

The victorious male, which was eagerly mounting the compliant female, sprang up into the air and then fell by the side of its would-be mate. It lay there twitching, its mostly white fur stained below the shoulder with blood.

Cimarron rose and as the female snowshoe bounded swiftly away into the forest, made his way toward his kill, holstering his gun as he went.

When he reached the rabbit and had made sure that it was dead, he went in the direction the fleeing female had taken and once within the stand of blackjack oak he broke off several dead branches from one of the trees and then searched until he found a pine. He got down on his knees, pulled his bowie knife from his boot, and probed the roots until he found what he had hoped to find—pitch. He scraped some of the gummy yellow substance from the roots and, balancing it on the blade of his bowie, carried it and the branches he had broken off back to where the rabbit lay lifeless.

He scraped the pitch from the knifeblade onto the surface of a stone and then proceeded to break short lengths off the branches. Using the knife, he whittled a series of shavings that curled outward but remained attached to the branches.

He crisscrossed several of the fuzz sticks he had made on a bare patch of ground and stood the others, tepee-fashion, above them. Then, after he had gripped a lock of his hair that brushed the collar of his buckskin jacket in his left hand, he used his knife to sever it.

He scraped the pitch from the stone and spread it on the fuzz sticks lying on the ground, and then he placed the lock of hair on top of the pitch.

He straightened, looked around, and then began to walk in an ever-widening circle, his eyes on the ground, searching for iron pyrites. He found none. But he finally did find a small piece of quartz, which he carried back and placed beside his tinder.

He hunkered down, picked up the limp body of the snowshoe, and lopped off its head and then its legs. He skinned and then gutted the animal, tossing its internal organs onto the pile that already contained the rabbit's head, legs, and hide.

He spitted the carcass with a length of one of the branches and then placed it on the grass. He picked up the piece of quartz he had found, unholstered his Colt, and striking downward along the barrel of the gun with the piece of quartz, caused several sparks to fall upon the tinder he had prepared.

They died before igniting the tinder, so he repeated the process; on his third try, he succeeded. He quickly dropped his gun and piece of quartz. Bending low, with his palms flat on the ground, he blew gently on the faintly smoking tinder. A tiny flame appeared. He continued blowing on it and a moment later, the lock of his hair and the pitch beneath it were burning smokily. Then the first of the fuzz sticks caught the fire and held it. When the flames were nearly a foot high, he fed more wood to the fire, and then, after holstering his Colt, he sat cross-legged on the ground, picked up the spitted rabbit, and held it over the flames.

Later, when the animal's flesh had turned crusty and the color of old gold, he withdrew it from the fire and, holding the spit by both ends, bit hungrily into the steaming flesh. He ignored the pain the hot meat sent searing through his lips and tongue as he tore large pieces of roasted flesh from the carcass and swallowed them after chewing them only slightly, his actions a testament to the hunger that had been ravening within him.

The sun had slipped below the western horizon when he finished eating and he sat, still cross-legged, on the ground and stared out across the land that was broken by cross timbers, letting their shadows settle on him as his fire burned low and finally went out.

He was still sitting in the same position, a pile of gristled bones by his boots, when the pale half-moon appeared in the sky, accompanied by the first of the night's bright stars.

He shivered as the wind rode over the land, got to his feet, and when he had gathered a number of evergreen branches, he used some of them to make a pallet on the ground beneath the trees. He sat down beside his makeshift bed, took off his hat, crumpled it, and placed it on the pine boughs to serve him as a pillow. He stretched out on the pallet he had made, and after unholstering his Colt and placing it beside his head, he pulled the remaining pine boughs over his body and curled up beneath them in an effort to escape the deep chill that had been sired on the dark night by the wildly roaming wind.

He closed his eyes and wrapped his arms around his body, listening to the silence. He heard it broken some minutes later by the faint *cheeping* of a field mouse in its nearby burrow. Later, he heard coyotes *yip-yipping* in the distance.

Just before he slipped down into a deep sleep, the face of Lyle Steen drifted up out of the darkness of his mind and he silently promised the man that they would meet again, and that their meeting, whenever and wherever it took place, would not be a pleasant one.

Dawn found Cimarron on his way to keep his promised rendezvous with Steen.

By the time he reached the eastern bank of the North Canadian River, his feet were badly blistered; by evening of the same day his blisters were bleeding, turning his socks into a warm wet swamp inside his boots.

That night he made a meal of bulrush root stalks that he dug out of the shallows of the river, and the following day just after noon he found a growth of wintergreen. He filled his pockets with the plants' spicy scarlet berries, eating some of them as he continued his journey northwest along the winding course of the North Canadian.

Two days later when he sighted Fort Supply on the western bank of the river, he slumped, exhausted, to the ground and stared at the tents that were lined up with proper military precision outside the fort's stockade and at the crowd of people, both soldiers and civilians, that had gathered near the fort's blockhouse. But his attention was not held for long by the crowd. It quickly turned to the large number of horses that were milling about in a rope corral just south of the blockhouse.

With his eyes still on the horses, he began to pull off his boots, a painful process, he soon discovered, and then he washed his bloody socks in the river. After spreading them on the wintry thatch of last summer's grass, he gingerly washed his feet, which were a mass of broken and bleeding blisters.

When he had eaten the last of the wintergreen berries, he rinsed the blood from inside his boots and put on his socks despite the fact that they were still wet, and then he pulled on his boots.

Later, as he walked along the bank searching for a place to ford the river, a wagon rumbled toward him from the east.

He turned toward the sound, and the wagon's driver hailed him. "Going to the trading yard?" the man called out cheerfully.

"Trading yard? They're trading horses at the fort?"

"Auctioning them off." The wagon driver gestured and Cimarron climbed up on the seat beside the man.

He listened to the driver's hope of "buying myself some good, if not exactly fine, stock" at the trading yard as they forded the river and drove toward the crowd clustered around the rope corral that contained the horses that were to be sold to the highest bidders.

"I'm much obliged to you for the ride," he told the wagon driver when they halted. He climbed down. "I hope you get what you came here after."

"Good luck to you, mister."

Cimarron made his way to the corral and stood with his hands in the back pockets of his jeans as he studied the horses that were to be offered for sale, keenly conscious of his money, which was missing because Steen had stolen his saddlebags.

No use my pining over what I can't have, he thought, and turned away from the corral.

His eye was immediately caught by a young woman who was wearing calfskin boots, a neat riding habit, and a low-crowned black hat with a chin loop. Without quite realizing what he was doing, he walked over to where she stood talking to a man who was showing her the quarter horse that stood beside him.

He halted a few steps away from the pair, his eyes on the woman. Her face was heart-shaped and pale. He noted her full lips, the lower one extended slightly in what might have been a pout as she listened to the man enthusiastically extol the virtues of his quarter horse. Her eyes were hazel and her hair was the same color, reaching almost to her shoulders in soft shining waves.

She's young, he thought. About nineteen. Maybe twenty. Twenty-one at the outside.

As the woman parted the lips of the quarter horse to examine its teeth, Cimarron studied the animal, and then, when the woman told the man beside her that she would try her best to buy the animal at the upcoming auction, he stepped up and touched a finger to his hat.

"You're in the market for an old-timer to ride, are you?" he asked her without preamble.

"No, I am not," she stated emphatically and with a trace of annoyance in her tone. "But this horse isn't an 'old-timer,' as you put it. Mr. Soames—he owns the animal—says he's just six years old."

"A lady like you oughtn't to be out buying horses till she's cut her trading teeth," he remarked.

"And what, may I ask, is that supposed to mean?" the woman snapped, her hands coming to rest on her hips as she stared haughtily at him, one of her booted feet tapping the ground.

He wet the tips of his fingers and ran them around the eyes and then over the ears of the quarter horse. He held them out to the woman so she could see the substance that stained them. "Potash," he explained. "A slick trader like Mr. Soames here uses it to cover up the gray hairs on an old horse he wants to make look younger so's he can unload it on somebody who don't know what she's doing—or buying.

184

"This mount's smooth-mouthed too. Guess you didn't notice that. I'll admit he's still pretty short in the tooth, but take yourself a look here." Cimarron opened the horse's mouth and, when the woman had stepped up to stand beside him, said, "Mr. Soames has gone and put cups in his teeth to try to hide his age—make him look a lot younger than he really is."

"I'm afraid I don't understand," the woman said tentatively.

"One way to make a horse look younger than he is— Well, what you do is you take a hot iron and heat the middle of his teeth to make them soft. Then you gouge out that part to make the cups. Then you rub a little nitrate of sugar into the cups and his teeth'll look real natural to even an experienced horse trader, which I take it you're not. There's one more thing worth mentioning. This horse is all grassed out."

"Grassed out?" The woman looked up at Cimarron, a frown wrinkling her forehead.

"Now, wait just a minute, mister, I—" Soames began.

But Cimarron, ignoring him, interrupted him. "This animal's eaten so much sand and gravel while grazing that his teeth are ground down real bad. He's what I said he is, grassed out."

"Why, you—"

As Soames swung on him, Cimarron gave the man a brutal right uppercut that sent him crashing to the ground, where he lay swearing and, despite Cimarron's urging, refusing to get up.

"I want to thank you for saving me from making a very bad investment," the woman told Cimarron, and before he could say anything more, she walked away and disappeared in the crowd.

He shrugged, and then, as the auctioneer took his place on a low wooden platform near the blockhouse, he joined the crowd and watched as horse after horse was brought to the platform and sold to the highest bidder.

At times, he searched the crowd for a glimpse of the woman who had intended to buy Soames' quarter horse, but he saw no sign of her.

I'm standing here, he thought, like one of those kings old Will Shakespeare wrote about. The one who'd've given his kingdom for a horse. Wish to hell I had some kind of kingdom to give for one right now.

When all the horses had been auctioned off, Cimarron was about to leave, but the auctioneer caught his and the crowd's attention with an announcement that he would now auction "various and sundry merchandise."

Cimarron watched as a crate of gobbling turkeys went on the block and then he turned and started to walk away. Suddenly, an idea flew full-blown into his mind. He quickly turned back, made his way around the edge of the crowd, and spoke urgently to the auctioneer, who, when he had finished speaking, frowned at him for a moment before breaking into a wide smile of pure pleasure.

"Gents!" he shouted. "I have here an extra-special item that will prove to be of real interest to all of you. I happen to have here a man who tells me he's temporarily down on his luck and in need of some cash to buy himself a horse and a few other things he's badly in need of.

"Now, what this man has just proposed to me is an idea I'd never have thought of myself. He proposes that I auction him off—for my usual ten percent of the bid price—as a hired hand to the highest bidder, for whom he's willing to work—and work hard, he assures me—until he can put together a decent grub stake for himself.

"Look at him, gents!" The auctioneer seized Cimarron by the arm and pulled him up onto the platform. "Strong as a young stallion, this man is, as you all can plainly see. Look at the powerful shoulders and arms he's got on him. Take a gander at that big-winded brisket of his and look at those legs that stand as strong as any Eyetalian marble."

The auctioneer reached down and seized Cimarron's wrists. Nodding his satisfaction, he continued, "Take yourselves a look as his hands." He held up Cimarron's hands, their palms facing the crowd. "Those calluses he's got are a sure sign he's a hardworking man, not a doubt about it. Now, then. Do I hear an opening bid for this bull's services?"

The auctioneer suddenly blushed and then, obviously flustered, said somewhat meekly, "I guess I'd best apologize to the ladies in the assemblage. I hope none of you mistook what I said about this man being a bull—or about, ah, his services. I meant merely to—"

"One dollar," a man in the crowd called out.

"One dollar," cried the auctioneer, releasing his hold on Cimarron's wrists and slapping a hand to his forehead in dramatic dismay. "Why, this big buck who stands here before you is worth ten at the very least!"

"Two dollars," a second bidder shouted.

"Three," countered the first bidder.

Cimarron began to smile when the competitive and spirited bidding quickly reached ten dollars. That's nine for me, he thought happily, and one for the auctioneer. Why, I'm already almost halfway to having a horse.

"Eleven," a man offered.

There was a long pause following his bid and then, "Twenty dollars!"

"Twenty," exulted the auctioneer. "Do I hear twenty-one? Twenty-one, anybody? No? Twenty once. Twenty twice. Sold to the lovely lady back there in the rear."

The woman Cimarron had met earlier made her way through the crowd and handed the auctioneer a double eagle. Then she turned and gave Cimarron a frankly appraising glance.

He gave her the same. And then he gave her a satisfied smile.

JOIN THE CIMARRON READER'S RANK

ABOUT THE AUTHOR

LEO P. KELLEY was born and raised in Pennsylvania's Wyoming Valley and spent a good part of his boyhood exploring the surrounding mountains, hunting and fishing. He served in the Army Security Agency as a cryptographer, and then went "on the road," working as dishwasher, laborer, etc. He later joined the Merchant Marine and sailed on tankers calling at Texan, South American, and Italian ports. In New York City he attended the New School for Social Research, receiving a BA in Literature. He worked in advertising, promotion, and marketing before leaving the business world to write full time.

Mr. Kelley has published a dozen novels and has several others now in the works. He has also published many short stories in leading magazines.

JOIN THE <u>CIMARRON</u> READER'S PANEL

If you're a reader of <u>CIMARRON</u>, New American Library wants to bring you more of the type of books you enjoy. For this reason we're asking you to join the <u>CIMARRON</u> Reader's Panel, so we can learn more about your reading tastes.

Please fill out and mail this questionnaire today. Your comments are appreciated.

1. The title of the last paperback book I bought was:
   TITLE:_____PUBLISHER:_____

2. How many paperback books have you bought for yourself in the last six months?
   ☐ 1 to 3   ☐ 4 to 6   ☐ 7 to 9   ☐ 10 to 20   ☐ 21 or more

3. What other paperback fiction have you read in the past six months?
   Please list titles: _____
   _____
   _____
   _____

4. My favorite is (one of the above or other): _____

5. My favorite author is: _____

6. I watch television, on average (check one):
   ☐ Over 4 hours a day ☐ 2 to 4 hours a day
   ☐ 0 to 2 hours a day
   I usually watch television (check one or more):
   ☐ 8 a.m. to 5 p.m.   ☐ 5 p.m. to 11 p.m.   ☐ 11 p.m. to 2 a.m.

7. I read the following numbers of different magazines regularly (check one):
   ☐ More than 6   ☐ 3 to 6 magazines   ☐ 0 to 2 magazines
   My favorite magazines are: _____
   _____

For our records, we need this information from all our Reader's Panel Members.

NAME:_____

ADDRESS:_____

CITY:_____STATE:_____ZIP CODE:_____

8. (Check one) ☐ Male   ☐ Female

9. Age (Check one): ☐ 17 and under   ☐ 18 to 34   ☐ 35 to 49
   ☐ 50 to 64   ☐ 65 and over

10. Education (check one):
    ☐ Now in high school   ☐ Graduated high school
    ☐ Now in college   ☐ Completed some college
    ☐ Graduated college

11. What is your occupation? (check one):
    ☐ Employed full-time ☐ Employed part-time ☐ Not employed
    Give your full job title:_____

Thank you. Please mail this today to:

CIMARRON, New American Library
1633 Broadway, New York, New York 10019

Exciting SIGNET Westerns by Ernest Haycox

Prices slightly higher in Canada

**Buy them at your local
bookstore or use coupon
on last page for ordering.**

SIGNET Westerns by Ray Hogan

(0451)

- [ ] **THE COPPER-DUN STUD** (125711—$2.25)*
- [ ] **THE RENEGADE GUN** (125215—$2.25)*
- [ ] **THE LAW AND LYNCHBURG** (121457—$2.25)*
- [ ] **THE RENEGADES** (119282—$2.25)*
- [ ] **DECISION AT DOUBTFUL CANYON** (111192—$1.95)*
- [ ] **THE DOOMSDAY BULLET** (116305—$1.95)*
- [ ] **LAWMAN'S CHOICE** (112164—$1.95)*
- [ ] **PILGRIM** (095766—$1.75)*
- [ ] **RAGAN'S LAW** (110307—$1.95)*
- [ ] **SIGNET DOUBLE WESTERN: OUTLAW MARSHAL and WOLF LAWMAN** (117441—$2.50)*
- [ ] **SIGNET DOUBLE WESTERN: MAN WITHOUT A GUN and CONGER'S WOMAN** (120205—$2.95)*
- [ ] **SIGNET DOUBLE WESTERN: BRANDON'S POSSE and THE HELL MERCHANT** (115910—$2.50)
- [ ] **SIGNET DOUBLE WESTERN: THREE CROSS and DEPUTY OF VIOLENCE** (116046—$2.50)
- [ ] **SIGNET DOUBLE WESTERN: DAY OF RECKONING and DEAD MAN ON A BLACK HORSE** (115236—$2.50)*
- [ ] **SIGNET DOUBLE WESTERN: THE VIGILANTE and THE REGULATOR** (124561—$2.95)*
- [ ] **SIGNET DOUBLE WESTERN: THE DOOMSDAY MARSHAL and THE DOOMSDAY POSSE** (126238—$2.95)*

*Prices slightly higher in Canada

Buy them at your local

bookstore or use coupon

on next page for ordering.

SIGNET Westerns by Lewis B. Patten

(0451)

- [ ] **VENGEANCE RIDER** (126211—$2.25)*
- [ ] **THE ANGRY HORSEMEN** (093097—$1.75)
- [ ] **A DEATH IN INDIAN WELLS** (112172—$1.95)*
- [ ] **POSSE FROM POISON CREEK** (095774—$1.75)
- [ ] **RED RUNS THE RIVER** (097378—$1.95)*
- [ ] **RIDE A TALL HORSE** (098161—$1.95)*
- [ ] **TRACK OF THE HUNTER** (110315—$1.95)*
- [ ] **THE TRAIL OF THE APACHE KID** (094662—$1.75)
- [ ] **SIGNET DOUBLE WESTERN: KILLING IN KIOWA and FUED AT CHIMNEY ROCK** (114256—$2.75)*
- [ ] **SIGNET DOUBLE WESTERN: SHOWDOWN AT MESILLA and THE TRIAL OF JUDAS WILLEY** (116313—$2.50)*
- [ ] **SIGNET DOUBLE WESTERN: REDSKIN and TWO FOR VENGEANCE** (119290—$2.75)*
- [ ] **SIGNET DOUBLE WESTERN: THE HIDE HUNTERS and OUTLAW CANYON** (122526—$2.95)*
- [ ] **SIGNET DOUBLE WESTERN: THE CHEYENNE POOL and THE TIRED GUN** (124928—$2.95)*
- [ ] **SIGNET DOUBLE WESTERN: DEATH STALKS YELLOWHORSE and THE ORPHANS OF COYOTE CREEK** (125223—$2.95)*
- [ ] **SIGNET DOUBLE WESTERN: AMBUSH AT SODA CREEK and MAN OUT-GUNNED** (125738—$2.95)*

*Prices slightly higher in Canada